NIGHT PEOPLE

BOOKS BY BARRY GIFFORD

FICTION

	Night People
The	Wild at Heart
Sailor & Lula	59° & Raining
Novels	Sailor's Holiday
	Sultans of Africa
	Consuelo's Kiss
	Bad Day for the Leopard Man

New Mysteries of Paris
A Good Man to Know
Port Tropique
Landscape with Traveler
An Unfortunate Woman
A Boy's Novel

NONFICTION

The Devil Thumbs a Ride & Other Unforgettable Films
A Day at the Races: The Education of a Racetracker
The Neighborhood of Baseball
Saroyan: A Biography (with Lawrence Lee)
Jack's Book: An Oral Biography of Jack Kerouac (with Lawrence Lee)

POETRY

Ghosts No Horse Can Carry: Collected Poems 1967–1987
Giotto's Circle
Beautiful Phantoms: Selected Poems
Persimmons: Poems for Paintings
Poems from Snail Hut
Horse hauling timber out of Hokkaido forest
The Boy You Have Always Loved
Coyote Tantras
The Blood of the Parade
Selected Poems of Francis Jammes (translations, with Bettina Dickie)

NIGHT PEOPLE

BARRY GIFFORD

GROVE PRESS • NEW YORK

Copyright © 1992 by Barry Gifford

Grove Press
841 Broadway
New York, NY 10003

Published in Canada by General Publishing Company, Ltd.

"Women Are Women but Men Are Something Else" was first published in *Buzz* (Los Angeles). "Everybody Got Their Own Idea of Home" appeared in the anthology *Love Is Strange: Stories of Post-Modern Romance* (New York).

Library of Congress Cataloging-in-Publication Data
Gifford, Barry, 1946–
Night people / Barry Gifford. —1st ed.
1. Title.
PS3557.I283N5   1992
813'.54—dc20   92-13449
ISBN 0-8021-3369-X (pbk.)

Manufactured in the United States of America

Designed by Kathy Kikkert

First Edition 1992

3 5 7 9 10 8 6 4 2

**THIS BOOK IS
FOR MY SISTER, RANDI,
WITH LOVE**

CONTENTS

There's something wild in the country
that only the night people know. . . .
—Tennessee Williams
Orpheus Descending

1

―

NIGHT PEOPLE

Women are impervious to evil.
—William Faulkner

APACHES

Big Betty Stalcup kissed Miss Cutie Early on the right earlobe as Cutie drove, tickling her, causing Cutie to swerve the black Dodge Monaco toward the right as she scratched at that side of her head.

"Dammit, Bet, you shouldn't ought do that while I'm wheelin'."

Big Betty laughed and said, "We're kissin' cousins, ain't we? Sometimes just I can't help myself and don't want to. Safety first ain't never been my motto."

Cutie straightened out the car and grinned. "Knowed that for a long time," she said.

"Knowed which? That we was kissin' cousins?"

"Uh uh, that come later. About the safe part. You weren't never very predictable, Bet, even as a child."

Big Betty and Miss Cutie had spent the week in New

Orleans, then the weekend in Gulf Shores, Alabama, and were headed back into Florida at Perdido Key. The Gulf of Mexico was smooth as glass this breezeless, sunny morning in February.

"Jesus H. Christ, Cutie, tomorrow's Valentine's Day!"

"So?"

"We'll have to make somethin' special happen."

"Last Valentine's we was locked up at Fort Sumatra. Spent the whole day bleachin' blood and piss stains outta sheets."

"Still can't believe we survived three and change in that pit."

"Don't know if I'd made it without you, Bet. Them big ol' mamas been usin' me for toilet paper, you weren't there to protect me."

Big Betty shifted her five-foot-eight, two-hundred-pound body around in the front passenger seat so that she faced Cutie Early. At twenty-four, Cutie was twelve years younger than Betty, and Miss Cutie's slim-figured five-foot-one-inch frame engendered in Big Betty a genuinely maternal feeling. They had been lovers ever since Miss Cutie had tiptoed into Big Betty's cell at the Fort Sumatra Detention Center for Wayward Women, which was located midway between Mexico Beach and Wewahitchka, Florida, just inside the central time zone. Cutie's curly red hair, freckles, giant black eyes and delicate features were just what Betty Stalcup had been looking for. It was as if the state of Florida penal system had taken her order and served it up on a platter. Big Betty brushed back her own shoulder-length brown hair with her left hand and placed her other hand on Cutie's right breast, massaging it gently.

"You're my baby black-eyed pea, that's for sure," said Betty. "We ain't never gonna be apart if I can help it."

"Suits me."

"Cutie, we just a couple Apaches ridin' wild on the lost highway, the one Hank Williams sung about."

"Don't know that I've ever heard of it."

"Travelin' along the way we are, without no home or reason to be or stay anywhere, that's what it means bein' on the lost highway. Most folks don't know what they want, Cutie, only mostly they don't even know that much. Sometimes they think they know but it's usually just their stomach or cunt or cock complainin'. They get fed or fucked and it's back to square one. Money makes 'em meaner'n shit, don't we already know. Money's the greatest excuse in the world for doin' dirt. But you and me can out-ugly the sumbitches, I reckon."

"How's that?"

"Just by puttin' two and two together, sweet pea, then subtractin' off the top, one at a time."

"I ain't sure I understand you, Bet, but I'm willin' to learn."

Big Betty threw back her head, shut her wolfslit green eyes and gave out a sharp laugh.

"Young and willin's the best time of life," she said. "You got to play it that way till you can't play it no more."

"Then what?" asked Cutie.

Big Betty grinned, threw her heavy left arm around Cutie's narrow shoulders and squeezed closer to her companion.

"Start cuttin' your losses," she said. "All that's left to do."

"Along with cuttin' throats, you mean."

"Why, Miss Cutie, honey, you way ahead of me."

CONDITIONS

Rollo Lamar leaned back in his oak swivel chair, lifted the red enamel Hopalong Cassidy cup to his lips and took a sip of Bustelo. He swished the hot black espresso around in his mouth awhile before swallowing it, then looked at Bobbie Dean. If he were a younger man, Rollo thought, he'd go for a slice of this. At sixty-four and counting, though, and six months past his quintuple bypass, Rollo let the notion slither by. He wasn't even supposed to be drinking coffee, let alone overdoing things with a delectable divorcée-to-be such as Bobbie Dean Baker.

Bobbie Dean had to be all of thirty now, Rollo figured. She'd buried two husbands before she turned twenty-five, and now here she was in his law office asking him to handle her divorce from number three. Bobbie Dean looked spectacular, he had to admit, with her white-blonde hair wrapped up around her head like a motel towel, blue shadow above and below her sparkly aqua eyes, long thin lips spread almost from one side of her face to the other, as if The Maker had begun to carve open her face like a grapefruit but stopped halfway. As Lightnin' Hopkins used to say, she was built up from the ground like a Coca-Cola bottle. Rollo Lamar lowered the coffee cup and placed it on his desk.

"I don't think we'll have any trouble with this, Bobbie Dean," Rollo said. "Your husband's income more than doubled both last year and this. Then there's Paisley Marie to think of. She's what, two now?"

"Be three next week."

"Won't prob'ly need to go to court, don't think. Leave it to me."

Bobbie Dean stood up, smiled sweetly at Rollo and let him eyeball her form for a bit.

"Bobbie Dean, you'd do wonders for a dead man."

Bobbie Dean laughed. "Don't know about a corpse, Mr. Lamar, but I'd like to think I got somethin' to do with improvin' a man's outlook on life, even temporarily."

After Bobbie Dean left, Rollo switched on the Admiral AM he'd had since he was a boy.

"This just out of Alice Springs, Australia," said the newsreader. "Aborigines attacked policemen with frozen kangaroo tails in a remote Northern Territory town and then ate the evidence, a court was told yesterday.

"Senior Constable Mark Coffey testified in Alice Springs court that the fifteen Aborigines bought the tails at a local store, then attacked three officers. Coffey said police believe the attack was motivated by an earlier attempt by police to move a man who was sitting in the middle of a highway in an apparent suicide bid. The man refused to move and a fight developed, Coffey said.

"After the attack on the policemen, six men were arrested and charged with assault. But a police spokesman said the kangaroo tails will not be introduced as evidence because it is believed they were eaten by the Aborigines."

Dumb shits, thought Rollo. That Abo probably plunked his ass down on the road because it was a sacred spot just happened to've been paved over. Damn cops anywhere would rather eliminate the indigenous population than try to understand them and work things out. Could have put a bend in the road there, for instance. All this time and they still ain't figured out there's an easier way.

Rollo Lamar picked up his Hoppy cup and drained the Bustelo. He closed his eyes, only dimly aware now of the droning radio. Before he'd gone under the knife, he'd made out his will, leaving virtually all of his assets to the American Heart Association, and provided for his burial, stipulating that the stone be engraved with the last words of Studs Lonigan, "Mother, it's getting dark." He thought of this now, and relaxed. A fitting epitaph for the world's condition, Rollo decided, and dozed off.

A GENERATION REMOVED

The two Peruvian seamen, brothers from Callao, Ernesto and Dagoberto Reyes, went straight from the *Madrugada,* a thirty-thousand-ton container ship registered in Liberia and berthed for eighteen hours at the Esplanade dock, to the Saturn Bar on the corner of St. Claude and Clouet in the Ninth Ward. Since Encanta's Tijuana, their former primary New Orleans hangout, had closed down two years before, the Reyes boys had frequented the Saturn—pronounced with the emphasis on the second syllable by the locals—whenever they hit town. It was a lively, though sometimes deadly little place, where the brothers could drink, dance with an assortment of neighborhood doxies and slumming college girls, shoot some pool and otherwise entertain themselves before heading back out to sea. This trip, the *Madrugada*'s next port of call was

Port of Spain, Trinidad, a place neither Ernesto nor Dagoberto cared much for, which is perhaps why they drank too many Abitas with Jim Beam chasers at the Saturn.

The two women they left with, the bartender, Bosco Brouillard, later told police, were strangers to him. One was large, Bosco said, about five-eight and heavy, even muscular, buxom, maybe in her late thirties. The other was small, just over five feet, boyish, pigeon-chested, a lot younger.

"Them ladies moved over those guys like Hypnos and Thanatos," said Bosco.

"Who're they?" asked the cop, who had discovered the butchered bodies of the Reyes brothers behind Swindle Ironworks on Burgundy over in the Eighth Ward.

"Sleep and Death," Bosco told him, "twin children of Nyx. You know, Night."

"No, I don't know," said the cop, who had not slept since he'd seen the pair of brown Peruvian heads hollowed out like cantaloupes scooped clean at a Cajun picnic.

"Gals had 'em covered, okay."

"Anyone else leave with them?"

The bartender shook his bald head no.

"Could be Morpheus was waitin' outside, though," Bosco said. "He's usually not far away."

"Who's this Morpheus?"

"The god of dreams, Nyx's sidekick. Say, you law-enforcement types ain't 'xactly up on your mythology, are ya?"

"Not really."

"Then I don't guess you know somethin' else is important."

The cop looked at the bartender, who was grinning now. The four television sets above the bar, each tuned to a different station with the sound off, flickered above his clean head.

"What's that?" the cop asked.

"Sleep, Dream and Death, they all only one generation removed from Chaos."

The policeman, whose name was Vernon Duke Douglas, and who was a direct descendant of H. Kyd Douglas, author of the book *I Rode with Stonewall,* folded his notepad and put it away.

"Obliged, Mr. Brouillard. We'll be around again, I'm certain."

Bosco winked his weak-lidded left eye at the Confederate scribe's great-great-great-nephew, and said, "Sir, I ain't no kind of travelin' man."

BEASTS IN THE JUNGLE

Big Betty and Cutie were lying on the double bed in their room in Jim & Jesse's Birth of a Nation Motel at Alligator Point. *Jaguar,* a Sabu movie made in 1956, was on the TV.

"This don't actually make whole bunches of sense," said Cutie, who lay on her stomach with her head at the foot of the bed. Her legs were bent at the knees and her feet twitched around each other.

"How's that, hon?" Big Betty asked. She was tired from driving all day, and had her eyes closed and her back and head propped up against two pillows next to the headboard.

"See, there's this ol' tribe of jaguar men lurkin' around and terrorizin' these oilfield workers in South America, right?"

"Yeah, so?"

"Then there's the young guy, Sabu, who left the tribe when he was a baby, and now the oilfield foreman is tryin' to trick him into thinkin' he—Sabu, I mean—is really revertin' to his natural self by gettin' into a kind of trance and then clawin' all these guys, but it's really the foreman in a jaguar suit who's doin' it."

"Why's that?"

"So the foreman can take over the project from the big boss, or somethin', I can't tell. Also, I figure the foreman's got the spotted hots for Chiquita, a native honey who's Sabu's soul-baby."

"Think I seen this one, Cutie. Bad guy gets eaten by piranhas at the end."

"Oh, wow, Bet! Now they got Sabu in a skin costume about to sacrifice some small squirmin' animal to the jaguar god, only he can't cut it. Look, now he thrown away the knife and had him a kind of fit. Chiquita takin' after him."

Betty opened her eyes and watched for a few seconds.

"Chick reminds me of that café au lait gal was in C block, Pearline Nail. You recall her?"

"Oh, yeah, sure do. She the one razored up Rupee Moreno when Rupee said a Baptist just someone don't favor lynchin' on Sunday."

Cutie got up and turned off the set. She picked up the copy of the *Tallahassee Democrat* that Betty had tossed on the floor and leafed through it.

"Hey, Bet, ain't this sweet as hell? Listen, this is in the 'Memorials' column of the newspaper: 'In loving memory of Blackie Lala. Born November 15, 1925—Died February 10, 1991. Pops, we can't forget you, we never will.

Oh, that cruel night you laid so still, we asked God why. Here's what he said, "He's with Me now, he's not dead. I know you loved him, so did I. I've taken him home, so please don't cry. Evil can destroy a man, it lurks in every corner. When love survives, as it surely can, pain lifts off the mourner." Sadly missed by his entire family. Signed, DeLeon, Felda, Birdie Dawn, Tequesta and Waldo Lala.' "

"Be somethin' different," Betty said, "havin' blood relatives means anything to ya. I never did."

Cutie put down the paper and curled up next to Big Betty's legs.

"There's blood between us, Bet, you know? It's how I feel."

Betty's right hand found Cutie's head and caressed it.

"I do know, sweet pea. You just the little lamb lyin' down with the ol' lion what's still got most her teeth."

"All I need, lady," Cutie said, and closed her eyes.

JUDGMENT

Other than the four years he'd spent as an undergraduate at the University of Chicago, and the four in New York while he had worked the counter at Hartley's Luncheonette on 116th Street and Amsterdam Avenue when he wasn't attending law school at Columbia, from which institution he received his degree, Rollo Lamar had spent his entire life in Egypt City, Florida.

His mother, Purity Mayfield, had worked as a maid for Arthur and Delia Lamar for ten years, from the time she was fifteen until she was twenty-five, at which age she died giving birth to her only child. Since the father, a juke joint piano player named Almost Johnson, was married to another woman and had been murdered in a mysterious incident soon after Purity's pregnancy became evident, and Purity Mayfield had no relatives in the vicinity, the Lamars, who were childless, adopted the boy and raised him as if he were their own son, even though they were white and he was black. They named him Rollo Mayfield Lamar, after Arthur's father and Rollo's mother.

The Lamar family had long been proponents of equal rights for all people, regardless of race or religion. Rollo Leander Lamar, Arthur's father, had been the first federal judge of the district in which Egypt City was situated, a position Arthur attained a generation later. Both Arthur and his father had attended Columbia Law, and so, of course, young Rollo followed suit.

Young Rollo, as he was known in Egypt City even into adulthood, was educated prior to his college years at home by Judge Lamar and his wife. Blacks were at that time not admitted to southern universities, other than exclusively colored institutions, so Young Rollo was sent to Chicago, a city he came to loathe. He spent his years there mostly sequestered in his dormitory room, studying, seldom venturing beyond the immediate area of the campus. New York he liked only a little better. Both places he found too cold, corrupt and unfriendly; the black people too aggressive. Rollo was relieved once his studies had been completed and he was able to return permanently to Egypt City.

Back home, he went to work for the firm of Lamar, Forthright & Lamar. Abe Forthright, Arthur Lamar's best friend and professional partner for twenty-seven years, had died of pleurisy shortly after Young Rollo's return, four years to the day after the Judge's fatal heart attack that occurred during the Miss Egypt City Beauty

Contest, of which the senior Lamar was, of course, a judge. Just as Breezy Pemberton strode onstage at the Gasparilla Livestock Center, wearing only a zebra-skin two-piece and ruby red spike heels, Judge Lamar keeled over sideways and fell off his chair. He was dead before he hit the ground, the doctor said, of a massive coronary.

Breezy Pemberton, who the following day was unanimously named by the four remaining judges as that year's Miss Egypt City, made this victory speech: "I'm entirely honored to have won but equally entirely horrified that my beauty might have caused the death of such a prominent citizen of our great town as Judge Lamar. I want the Lamar family to know that it never was any intention of my own to upset the Judge by wearin' a zebra two-piece, certainly not to inspire such a terrible tragedy as has occurred. But I guess sometimes this kinda thing happens, whether required by God or not of course I am in no position to understand, and it ain't no person's fault. I am sixteen-and-one-half years old and Judge Lamar was much, much older, I know, and seein' a young lady, namely me, like that caused a shock to his tired-out system he was no longer capable of standin', and it's too bad. I'm sorry for the Lamars that is left, but I'm also thrilled to've won the title of Miss Egypt City on my first try, and I just want to say I'm dedicatin' my reign to the mem'ry of the dead judge. Thank you all, you're very sweet."

Rollo was accepted by the community as a Lamar and treated, as far as he could tell, like any other man, despite the fact of his being black. There were very few black citizens of Egypt City, the population of which remained constant at approximately 15,000. Rollo had never married, living on alone in the Lamar house after Delia's death. Delia had kept a signed photograph of Breezy Pemberton, which Breezy had presented to her in a gold-edged frame, on the piano in the front room for several years, but as soon as the news reached Egypt City that Breezy had died of acute alcohol poisoning in a room at the Las Sombras Motel in Hermosa Beach, California, Delia took the photo, frame and all, and threw it into the trashbin.

"Why'd you do that, Mama?" Rollo had asked her.

"For every good reason, Son," Delia said.

CONFLUENCE

In 1934, Rollo Leander Lamar had been the founder of the Colored Waifs' Home on Trocadero Island. Thirty years later, following passage of the Civil Rights Act, the Home was renamed the R. L. Lamar Orphanage for Florida's Destitute Tots. Young Rollo made regular visits to FDT, as it was called, usually on the third Saturday of every month.

On this particular Saturday, Rollo rolled his aqua Chrysler New Yorker onto State Highway 98 at twenty minutes past ten in the morning, expecting to reach Trocadero Island before noon. The sky was overcast but Rollo wore sunglasses anyway, out of habit. He switched on the radio.

"And from Miami comes the news that Piero Turino has died at the age of sixty-two. Mr. Turino, an explorer who conquered the Andes, survived machine gun wounds and an attack by flesh-eating fish, succumbed to a heart attack.

"A European count who inherited but did not use the title, Turino was born in Istria, which became part of Yugoslavia. His latest venture had been in the field of medical research involving substances he had brought back from the Amazon, which he believed embodied anti-cancer properties.

"In 1940, Turino, then a teenage soldier in the Italian army, was machine-gunned near the Greek border during the Balkan campaign. Wounded in the chest, he was taken to Albania and placed on a hospital ship bound for Italy. Halfway across the Adriatic, the ship was sunk by a submarine. Turino again survived, rescued from the sea by a passing ship.

"In the late 1940s, he emigrated to Canada, where he became a writer and broadcast journalist. Later he invented the Turino Control-Descent Parachute, used by the U.S. government, and once survived a test jump that landed him in the middle of a Boston freeway.

"Piero Turino and his wife moved to Miami in the mid-1960s, and soon thereafter he began his expeditions in South America. While diving in a murky pool in the jungles of Venezuela, he was attacked by fish that tore apart his left hand and wrist. The intrepid Turino suffered profuse bleeding and delirium, but survived. His widow, Isabella Lanapoppi Turino, reported that his last words were, 'My advice is to survive as long as possible, because when you die, you vanish. A man will never be remembered as he truly was.'"

"No good goddamn reason he should be, either," Rollo said aloud.

A commercial came on so Rollo reached down and switched the dial to another station. "My girl," sang The Temptations, "talkin' 'bout my girl." Rollo left it there.

Big Betty and Cutie had awakened early that morning, made love, showered together, dressed, packed up and checked out of the motel.

"We'll get coffee on the road, Cutie, okay?" Big Betty said as they got into the black Monaco. "There's some cupcakes left over in the back, you want 'em."

"Ain't particularly hungry, Bet, thanks. Where we headed, anyway?"

"Trocadero Island, place I always wanted to see. Have a bird sanctuary there. Also figure it's time we got back to work, sweet pea, don't you think?"

"Cleanin' up for the Lord."

Betty laughed. "Yeah, She likes things orderly."

MISS CUTIE, HER EARLY LIFE

Cutie Early was born in Daytime, Arkansas, population 1150, to Naureen (née Harder) and Arlen "Left" Early. Soon after her birth, Cutie moved with her parents to Plant City, Florida, where Arlen found work as a bridgetender on the Seabord Rail Line. Over the next four years, two more children followed: a boy, Ewell, called You, and another girl, Licorice. Being the eldest, it fell to Cutie to tend her siblings as soon as she was able, especially after Naureen developed an unfortunate affection for Southern Comfort.

At about the same time that his wife found a friend in a bottle, Arlen found one across town, a divorcée named Vanna Munck, with whom he soon kept more than casual company. When Cutie was ten, her daddy left the family and went to live with the Munck woman. One year later, at suppertime, Naureen drove her yellow Voláre over to Vanna Munck's house and left it idling in front while she went inside and shot Left Early and his paramour to death with a .38 caliber handgun her delinquent husband had given her to protect herself with when she was alone in the house. After murdering Arlen and Vanna, Naureen, who was apparently stone-cold sober at the time, got back into her vehicle and drove it as fast as it would go smack into a brick wall behind the Reach Deep Baptist Church. The police concluded that she had died practically on impact.

The children were taken in by Arlen's brother, Tooker, and his wife, Fairlee, who lived in Tampa. You and Licorice accomplished a relatively seamless transition, but Cutie had difficulty adjusting. Her first serious misstep occurred when she was twelve-and-a-half years old. Cutie had been on a date with a Cuban boy named Malo Suerte, who was seventeen, and they had driven in Malo's Mercury through the exit at the Seminole Outdoor Auto Theater. The drive-in security cop, Turp Puhl, a former prison guard at Starke, had a particular hatred for kids who tried to sneak in without paying. After spotting the red Merc as it crept stealthily with its lights off toward a vacant stall, Turp Puhl pulled out his revolver and made a beeline for the intruder.

As soon as the illegal entrant was berthed, the security guard ordered Malo and Cutie out at gunpoint. Malo swung the driver's-side door hard into Turp, who dropped his revolver. While the boy and the man struggled, Cutie came around the rear of the Mercury, picked up the fallen weapon, and shot Turp Puhl once behind his left knee, causing him to curse loudly and release his grip on Malo. Malo grabbed the gun from Cutie, jumped back into his car and drove away, leaving Cutie standing next to the wounded guard, who took hold of the girl and held on to her until the police arrived.

Cutie was sent to the Nabokov Juvenile Depository for Females at Thanatossa for eighteen months. Shortly thereafter, Malo Suerte went off the Gandy Bridge and drowned in his Mercury after it blew a front tire while being chased by the highway patrol.

By the time she was sixteen, Cutie had established herself as a regular problem, for both her family and the Tampa police. You and Licorice loved her, but they had their own little lives to sort out, so they kept their distance. After Tooker discovered a cache of knives, including a Hibben Double Shadow dagger, a fifteen-inch Mamba, a quarter-inch-thick Gurkha MK3 and several Italian switchblades, under Cutie's bed, he confiscated the weapons and turned them in, along with Cutie, to the authorities. The knives had been stolen by a boyfriend of hers named Harley Reel, a part-time shrimp salesman who lived with his wife and four children in a trailer home in Oldsmar. He had asked Cutie to keep the knives for him until he found a customer. Harley Reel got four years in Raiford, and Cutie, whom Tooker and Fairlee told the judge they never wanted to see again, was sent back to Thanatossa until she turned eighteen.

Since then, Cutie had supported herself mostly by waitressing, with some soft-hooking thrown in. Her definition of a soft-hooker was a girl who worked without a pimp and made dates privately, without advertising or standing on a corner. Cutie usually went out with older men who didn't mind paying for her time. Most of them couldn't get it up anyway, Cutie found out, which made her job easier, although occasionally a john's frustration over his inability to perform caused him to physically abuse her. Cutie quickly learned to take the money at the beginning of the evening, which ordinarily included dinner, rather than have to go through what could be a difficult scene afterwards. Working without a pimp to protect her had its drawbacks, but Cutie liked not having to be responsible to anyone other than herself.

Cutie had ended up at Fort Sumatra after a bad date, during which she'd been forced to stick a customer in the ribs with a Tanto boot knife. The john had paid Cutie a hundred dollars for letting him piss on her hair. Ordinarily, she didn't do perv, but this was an old guy, in his seventies, he seemed nice, and he promised not to get any urine on her face. He lost control and sprayed her all over, and she jumped up before he'd finished, which angered him. The old man began beating on her, so Cutie cut him. There just happened to be a cop standing outside the motel room when the stuck customer started screaming and Cutie, still dripping wet from the golden shower, ran out.

Big Betty looked out for her now. Cutie knew she could trust her, they could trust each other, and that, Cutie felt, was about the most one woman could ever hope to expect from another. Men hadn't even progressed that far, she figured, and now it was too late. She and Bet were at the end of their rope with them.

BIG BETTY, HOW IT HAPPENED

Dubuque "Big Boy" Stalcup, Betty's father, was fully grown at six-foot-six, two hundred thirty-five pounds by the time he was sixteen. He was raised on a south Georgia farm next to the Suwanoochee Creek close to the point at which the Suwannee River crawls out of the Okefenokee Swamp. The Stalcup place wasn't so much a farm, really, as a junkyard hideout for criminals. Big Boy's father and mother, Mayo and Hilda Sapp, maintained an infamous safe house for thieves, moonshiners and killers on the run. Whenever the law got up enough nerve to invade the Stalcup sanctuary, which was not often, the various fugitives in residence used a secret trail to the swamp, where they would remain until one of the Stalcup kids came to tell them it was safe to come back. The Stalcups made no real attempt to work their land, which had been homesteaded in 1850. The War Between the States passed the Stalcup clan by; they were too remote and the males considered extraordinarily crazy and too danger-ous by those few who were acquainted with them to be pressed into service of the Confederacy.

Big Boy and his wife, Ella Dukes, had four children, of which Betty was the youngest and also the only girl. Her three brothers, Sphinx, Chimera and Gryphon—each of whose names were chosen by Big Boy from *Bulfinch's Mythology,* the only book other than the Bible that he owned—never left the farm. Betty, named by Ella after her grandmama, Elizabeth Hispaniola, a niece of the Seminole warlord Osceola, had run off at the age of fourteen with Duval and Sordida Head, a brother and sister from Cross City, Florida, who had robbed a bank in Valdosta and paid the Stalcups to hide them. Their descriptions of city life intrigued Betty, and she agreed to leave with them when they felt the time was right. Betty never said goodbye to her parents or brothers and never returned to the farm.

After Duval had used her several times, he tired of Betty and passed her to his sister, whose sexual proclivi-ties involved mainly the participation of women and dogs. Sordida introduced the adolescent Betty, who at fourteen was already a rather large person, to the de-lights of female love, which Betty found preferable to the rough ways of the men who had handled her—namely her brothers, who had deflowered their sister when she was nine and subsequently took their pleasure with her whenever one or more of them felt the urge, and Duval Head. Betty told Sordida that Sphinx, Chimera and Gryphon really preferred cornholing one another anyway, and figured she'd hardly be missed.

Big Betty stayed with the Heads for a few months, during which time they knocked off dozens of convenience stores and gas stations and burglarized homes all over the state of Florida. Duval and Sordida went off one day to rob a bank in Fort Walton Beach, leaving Betty to wait for them in the Greyhound bus station, and they never returned. A man and his wife who were traveling to Miami gave Betty enough money for a ticket to New Orleans, a city that for no reason she could think of Betty told the couple was her destination. Betty never did learn that both Duval and Sordida had been killed in a head-on crash with an eighteen-wheel Peterbilt transporting commodes when Duval drove their 1972 Dodge Coronet onto an off ramp of Interstate 10 while attempting to elude a police car in hot pursuit.

Betty found work in New Orleans as an exotic dancer at the Club Spasm on Opelousas Avenue in Algiers. She was big enough to pass for twenty-one and nobody questioned her. Between her dancing gig and turning occasional tricks on the side, Betty did all right. She stayed away from drugs and alcohol, neither of which particularly agreed with her, and entered into a series of lesbian relationships with other dancers and prostitutes. Many of the women with whom Betty consorted were married or had boyfriends, a situation to Betty's liking; she was not interested in committing herself to any one person and discovered that she enjoyed living alone. Privacy, a condition she had never truly experienced either at home or on the road with the Heads, was her greatest pleasure.

Eventually, Betty moved on to Houston, then Dallas,

where she took a small caliber bullet in her left ankle from a drunken patron named Feo Lengua, an illegal from Nueva Rosita, while she was dancing onstage at Rough Harvey's Have Faith Sho-Bar. After she was shot, Betty's days as an exotic dancer were finished, and she worked as a bartender, card dealer, waitress, seamstress, car wash cashier and hooker—just about anything and everything, as she drifted from Texas back through Louisiana and Mississippi to Alabama and Florida.

It was in Orlando, where she was working in a janitorial capacity, cleaning up a medical building after hours, that Betty was brutally raped and beaten by two male co-workers one night on the job. Betty reported the attack to the police, who several days later informed her that there was insufficient evidence to pursue the case. She bought a Beretta .25 caliber automatic at Emmett's Swap City off the Orange Blossom Trail near the Tupperware International headquarters, went to the apartment of one of her assailants, a glue-sniffing freak named Drifton Fark, found him in an olfactory stupor, and shot him just below the heart. She then hunted down Drifton Fark's companion, Willie "Call Me Israel" Slocumb, a black man who claimed to be a Miccosukee Indian and who had converted from Disciples of Christ to Judaism after reading Sammy Davis, Jr.'s account of his own conversion in his autobiography, *Yes I Can!*, and shot him once in the right knee and again in the groin while he sat at the bar in The Blind Shall Lead Lounge across from the Flying Tigers Warbird Air Museum.

After Betty shot Willie "Call Me Israel" Slocumb and

watched him drop to the floor, writhing in pain and clutching at his affected parts, she laid the Beretta on the bar and told the bartender to call the cops. She sat down on the stool next to the one that had been occupied by her most recent victim, picked up the glass he had been about to drink from prior to the interruption, and drained the contents, a double shot of Johnny Walker Black on the rocks. Just before the police arrived, Betty told the bartender, "You know, that's the first time liquor really tasted decent to me."

Betty was sent to the Fort Sumatra Detention Center for Wayward Women, where, until she met up with Cutie Early, she kept mostly to herself. Miss Cutie was the one for her, all right, Betty decided, the only person she could rely on forever and ever, her ideal friend. Betty had an agenda, of course, but Cutie, Big Betty vowed, would always rate just as high on the big chart of life as she did herself.

EVERYBODY GOT THEIR OWN IDEA OF HOME

As Rollo Lamar drove toward Trocadero Island, he thought about B. Traven, the writer who had insisted on keeping the details of his life, including his birth, real name and heritage, secret so long as he was alive. Rollo, who had always been a dedicated reader of fiction, was a great admirer of Traven's work, such as *The Treasure of the Sierra Madre; The Death Ship; The Cotton-Pickers;* his jungle series, which included the novels *March to the Montería, The General from the Jungle, Government* and *The Carreta;* and many others.

Traven had deliberately attempted to cover his tracks, with good reason, since he had been a radical journalist and activist in his native Germany and become a wanted man there. He escaped to Mexico, changed his name more than once, worked as a mer-

chant seaman and in the mahogany forests, finally mar-
rying and settling down to the life of a novelist and
short-story writer in Mexico City. Traven and his wife
raised two daughters there, and when director John
Huston made a film of *Treasure,* starring Humphrey Bo-
gart, Traven received a certain amount of notoriety,
even though he attempted to masquerade, during his
stint as technical advisor to the production, as a friend
of Traven's named Hal Croves.

Rollo liked not only Traven's novels but his repeated
statements that the man who produced the work was of
no real importance, that only the work should be exam-
ined, not the life of the author. Of course, Traven was
paranoid, concerned that his early life and supposed
crimes might be revealed. Whether or not he would still
have been held accountable for any incendiary acts was
doubtful; nevertheless, "the man nobody knows," as he
fictionalized himself, developed a strict philosophy
based on the insignificance of the creator.

It made sense to Rollo, and as he wheeled along he
decided that it would not be the worst condition in the
world to become utterly anonymous, known only to one-
self. That way, the truth would disappear and there
would remain only the brutal evidence of a life, the
greater truth, without the unnecessary pain of reexami-
nation. Life itself is difficult enough, Rollo thought. Ret-
rospective investigation, Traven knew, could reveal
nothing of real value, so he did his best to conceal his
origin. It was a difficult maneuver, given the amount and
quality of the work he produced, and the fact that it was
intended for public consumption.

Rollo, who at sixty-four bore an uncanny resemblance, though of darker hue, to the actor Broderick Crawford as he appeared in the 1955 movie *Big House, U.S.A.,* had no desire nor any reason to disappear. There was nothing in his past he needed to cover up. In fact, he realized, his life had been rather dull, marked by no really emotionally searing events, despite the death of his mother when he was a young boy and unusual circumstances of his subsequent upbringing by the Lamars. He had no responsibilities other than to himself, and no outstanding complaints. As he headed his car across the Trocadero Island Bridge, he wondered if it was too late for things to change.

Once across the bridge, Rollo pulled into the yard in front of Jasper Pasco's Fishin' Pier and Grocery, a regular stop of his on this run. Rollo needed to stretch his legs, and he usually enjoyed his visits with Jasper Pasco, whom Rollo had known since the Judge started taking him along on trips to the orphanage fifty-three years before. Jasper had to be at least eighty-eight now, Rollo figured, but still more than able and willing to carry both ends of a conversation without much encouragement.

Rollo stretched his arms and legs, bent over at the waist as best he could and then walked into the store. Before the screen door could bang shut behind Rollo, Jasper was at him.

"You look like a man in need of a ringer for squeezin' meat from a muskrat," the old man shouted from his perch on a high stool behind a wooden counter laden with a motley assortment of items, such as purple tennis shoes, a bucket of used golf balls, net dip for treating trawls, loaves of Wonder Bread, all sizes and varieties of nails, red potatoes, an LP album of Conway Twitty's greatest hits, green Red Man tobacco baseball caps and more. Behind Jasper on the wall was a nine-by-twelve-inch framed photograph of John F. Kennedy, autographed by the slain president and inscribed, "To J. Pasco, for whom may the catfish continue to bite and bite hard."

"Lost my taste for muskrat when I was a boy," Rollo said.

"Then I guess to hell you're after chicken necks," said Jasper, "you're goin' fishin'."

"No, thanks, Jasper. I'm on my way to check on the orphans, as usual. See they ain't bein' made to sleep on their same pee-stained sheets nights."

Jasper grunted. "Ain't wet the bed myself since my pecker seized up six, seven years back. Used to be I was only full of vinegar, now I'm full of piss and vinegar. Haw!"

Rollo smiled and shook Pasco's liver-spotted right hand. Jasper reached down with his left and massaged his bare left foot.

"Got the athlete's foot, Rollo. Doctor told me wear socks, but I hate 'em. Hate wearin' socks almost as much as I hate most my neighbors abandoned me for the Piggly Wiggly soon as it went in up the highway. I used to be a sweet fella, Rollo, you knew me about when. Then that lyin' sumbitch Scaramouche, when he was state senator, promised me the game warden's job if I swung the local vote his way, never come through. That was the start of my bad luck, okay. He gone up to Washington with the U.S. Congress, asked him to pre-vent the Piggly Wiggly comin' in, ruinin' my business, but the sumbitch never even wrote me back. Wouldn't take my phone calls, neither. Well, I ain't easygoin' no more, you can bet. I'm gonna laugh lastest and longest, though. You'll see."

"Oh, Jasper, shut," said a thin, eagle-beaked woman sitting on another stool behind the counter. She was smoking an unfiltered cigarette and looked to be about ten or fifteen years Jasper's junior.

"Hello, Hermina," Rollo said to old man Pasco's wife of forty-six years. "How you been keepin'?"

Hermina emitted her version of laughter, an extended screech, which sounded as if she had unexpectedly been doused with a bucket of ice water.

"Protectin' this jackass from himself is about all I ever do," said Hermina. "No man on earth better suited to guaranteein' grief to a body than Mr. Pasco, you know it."

"What you expect, the world decayin' the way it is?" Jasper shouted. "Can't expect people to keep a promise! Look at that truck passin' there," he said, pointing at the road. "Shrimper with a butterfly net. Butterfly nets are the ruination of human creation! Can't get the re-frigerator man to come out. Tobacco man shows late. Remar the cracker man ain't been in two weeks. And Bowlegs Linda the cupcake girl we ain't seen since she went to Pensacola to bury her mama."

"Bury her mama, my bony ass," said Hermina. "That girl gettin' buried under by the navy, is what."

"I been around," Jasper said. "Dogpatch USA, Six Flags Over Texas, Rock City, Disney World. Ain't much I haven't seen. Had me a Co-Cola once with Connie Francis in Dothan, Alabama. Or was it a beer with Crystal Gayle in Calhoun, Georgia? Which was it, Hermina?"

Hermina screeched and coughed, expelling a small cloud of cigarette smoke as she did.

"Go on and laugh, woman! Rollo, you ask people up and down the Gulf Coast about this place and if they don't know me they ain't never been a cow in Texas."

"Just stopped by to say hello, Jasper," Rollo said, "and to pick up a roll of Spear-o-mint Lifesavers, you got any."

Jasper reached into a pile, fished around and came up with something.

"Only got Pep-o-mint," he said.

"Good enough," said Rollo, taking the candy from Jasper and handing him four bits.

" 'Preciate it, Rollo. You come by again soonest."

"Next time I'm here, Jasper. Take care, now. You too, Hermina."

Jasper's wife sat and smoked. Wrinkled, sagging skin hooded her eyes.

"Everybody got their own idea of home," she said.

Rollo walked to his car, unwrapping the Lifesavers as he proceeded, popped one into his mouth and was about to get in when a voice behind him inquired, "Mister, you believe the devil needs a witness?"

Rollo turned around and saw a large, dough-faced woman with small pink eyes standing there, holding a gun in her right hand. She pointed it at Rollo's belly.

"It's okay, honey," Big Betty said, "you can drive."

Betty opened the driver's door, got in and slid over to the front passenger seat.

"Come on, get in," she ordered, and Rollo obeyed, dropping the roll of Lifesavers on the ground as he did.

"Well, what do you think?" she asked, as Rollo started the car and put it in gear.

"About what?"

"The devil needin' a witness."

"I wouldn't know."

"You will," said Big Betty.

BEDBUGS

Cutie kept the black Monaco close behind the aqua New Yorker as the vehicles proceeded in tandem past the turnoff for the R. L. Lamar Orphanage for Florida's Destitute Tots. In the Chrysler, Big Betty pushed the nose of her revolver up against Rollo's right kneecap as he drove, following her directions. Rollo did not ask any questions. He thought about Bobbie Dean Baker, how she looked standing in his office the day before, and decided that if he survived this situation, whatever it turned out to be, he would definitely do his best to turn a professional relationship into a personal one. Bobbie Dean was between marriages, after all, and she certainly was friendly. There weren't many women of any age in Egypt City, Rollo thought, who had a shape as fine as Bobbie Dean Baker's. He wondered if she'd heard about his quintuple bypass and whether that information would work in his favor or not. Finally, his curiosity got the best of him.

"I trust you won't mind my asking you what this is all about," Rollo said.

"Trust is what it's all about, all right," Big Betty answered. "Turn left up here."

Rollo did as she instructed and noticed the dark Dodge sticking to his Chrysler's tail.

"Keep on now straight the next ten miles, then I tell you how to go."

"You connected to that person following us?"

Betty laughed. "All ways exceptin' at the navel. You ever hear about them twins in Belle Fourche, South Dakota? Darlene and Delores."

"What about them?"

"They was prob'ly close as me'n Cutie. By the way, my name's Betty Stalcup. Yours?"

"Rollo Lamar."

"Glad to know ya, Rollo. You're not bad lookin' for a older type, coffee-colored fella. Anyway, these gals in Belle Fourche was charged with murderin' a man each sister had married twice. I got the newspaper clippin' here, you want to know the details."

"I don't guess I'd mind."

Big Betty took the article from her shirt pocket, unfolded the paper and began reading:

" 'Jurors convicted one woman of conspiracy to commit first-degree murder but acquitted her twin sister of charges that they helped to kill the eighty-five-year-old man each had married twice.'

" 'Darlene Phillips was convicted of the most serious

charge but cleared of all other charges. Her sister, Delores Christenson, was acquitted of all charges. Phillips received mandatory life in prison.'

" 'Phillips and Christenson, forty-six, have each been married four times. Both had brushes with the law before they were indicted in the death of Walter Gibbs, who was slain April Fools' Day 1990 at his home in Lemmon.'

" ' "Walter was a nice guy until he got mixed up with those nitwit twins," said Lillian Burns of Morristown, whose husband, George, was a close friend of Gibbs. "They're crazier than a couple of bedbugs." '

" 'Jerome Phillips, thirty-eight, a convicted rustler who is married to Darlene but says he is in love with her sister, confessed to smothering Gibbs with a pillow. He testified at the twins' trial this week that Darlene helped hold down Gibbs. Phillips pleaded guilty May twenty-first to a murder conspiracy charge. He is to be sentenced next month.'

" 'The twins had been charged with planning the murder and helping to kill the frail Gibbs. Phillips said he and the twins had several discussions about ways to kill Gibbs, who had named Christenson as heir to his $178,000 estate.'

" 'Bob Van Norman, who represented Christenson, told the jury that his client essentially has the mental capacity of a second-grader and is not nearly smart enough to either plan Gibbs's death or to know that she should report the murder scheme to authorities.' "

"Course this is where me'n Cutie differs from them," Big Betty interjected, before continuing with the arti-

cle: " 'Gibbs was fifty-eight when he first married Christenson, who was eighteen at the time. They were di-
vorced about ten years later, and he married Darlene.
Another divorce, two remarriages to the twins and one
other marriage brought his total to five marriages.'

" ' "It's confusing to everybody who knows them,"
Burns said.'

" 'Darlene Phillips is already serving a fifty-year
prison term for trying to burn down Gibbs's farmhouse
in 1989 while he was sleeping on the couch. A neighbor
saw the fire and helped Gibbs get out. She was sentenced
on the arson conviction in August 1990, four months
after Gibbs's death.'

" 'Authorities first thought Gibbs's death was natural
but got suspicious several months later when they received a tip that Darlene Phillips was blabbing in prison
about a murder. Gibbs's body was exhumed thirteen
months after burial. Officials had thought he died at the
hospital in Lemmon, a town of 1,600 in northwestern
South Dakota, just three blocks from the North Dakota
line. Although his body was taken to the hospital, they
did not discover until later that he was dead when an
ambulance picked him up.'

" 'Jerome Phillips is serving eight years for rustling
sheep and pigs last year. Christenson served sixty days
for helping him. Darlene Phillips met her present husband in the state's prison for men and women several
years ago when she was serving time for torching a
house in Bison and he was in jail for writing bad
checks.'

" ' "The twins tell me I'm like a brother to them," said

Lemmon Police Chief Nick Schaefer. "I don't know why, because I've arrested them several times." ' "

"You and this Cutie got some philosophy in common with these women, you say?" asked Rollo.

"Don't know much about philosophy," said Big Betty, "but it's not strictly a man's world no longer, or ain't you noticed?"

She spotted a faded wooden road sign that said TROCADERO ISLAND ROD & GUN CLUB — MEMBERS ONLY.

"Pull in here," Betty commanded. "End of the line."

THE LAIR

The Trocadero Island Rod & Gun Club building had been abandoned for seventeen years, ever since a privately chartered bus carrying all thirty-two of the club's members had gone off the Trocadero Island Bridge into the Gulf of Mexico. The driver, a fifty-three-year-old one-eyed Honduran citizen named Eusebio Refrito, had fallen asleep at the wheel shortly past midnight of the day the members were returning from the club's annual "Live Free or Why Die?" weekend in New Orleans. Virtually all of them were in a drunken stupor when the bus flipped over the guard rail.

Everyone aboard drowned, including Eusebio Refrito, who had dozed off while half-dreaming about his seventeen-year-old second cousin, Nefaria Reina, who was still living in Tegucigalpa, and with whom Eusebio had begun having sexual relations when she was twelve and he was forty-eight. He had not seen Nefaria for seven months, since Eusebio had fled the economic disaster area his country had become and illegally entered the United States in a SAHSA ("Stay at home, stay alive") jet at the Miami airport inside of a packing crate otherwise filled with machetes. At the moment the nose of the two-million-mile veteran of America's highways hit the bridge railing, Refrito was fantasizing Nefaria half-undressed, running the violet tip of her tongue along the popping purple vein of his ruler-length penis. *"Mi prima!"* Eusebio shouted a millisecond past impact, not knowing that his spinal cord already had been severed.

Big Betty and Cutie had moved into the Rod & Gun Club the night before they snatched Rollo Lamar. Betty made Rollo precede her and Cutie into the building. There was nothing in the large front room but the women's bedrolls, a camp stove and cooking gear.

"Why am I here?" Rollo asked.

"Aaron stretched out his hand with his rod and smote the dust of the earth, and it became lice," said Cutie. "All the dust of the land became lice throughout all the land of Egyp'. That's from Exodus."

"Men are lice," said Betty. "You're our own private experiment in reeducation, Mr. Lamar. We're gonna see if we can make one man right with the Lord before the sword does its swift work."

"Except a man be born again, he cannot see the kingdom of God," said Cutie.

Big Betty nodded and chorused: "Nicodemus saith unto Him: 'How can a man be born when he is old? Can

45

he enter the second time into his mother's womb and be born?' "

Cutie closed her eyes, continuing: "Jesus answered . . . 'Marvel not that I said unto thee, "Ye must be born again." ' That's St. John."

"My lord," said Rollo.

Big Betty hit him on the left side of his head with her gun, knocking Rollo to the floor.

"You ain't got no claim, Mr. Lamar," she explained. "It don't nearly work that way. As Elmer Ernest South-ard said in *The Kingdom of Evils,* before you get the Grail, you got to slay the dragon."

WAVELAND, MISSISSIPPI

"Recall once seein' a girl was struck by lightnin' on the beach at Waveland, Miss'ippi," said Cutie. "She was maybe 'bout ten, which's close to my age at the time. Saw she was helpin' her family load their beach belongin's back of their car when the bolt hit her. Knocked a bucket straight out her hand. Fried the girl coulda been me."

It was two A.M. and Big Betty and Cutie were lying together in a double bag. Their portable shortwave was on, tuned in to an FM station. Clyde McPhatter was singing "Warm Me Up" in his smooth falsetto. Rollo was asleep in the extra bag twenty feet away.

"That must been terrifyin' for you, sweet pea, bein' so young and impressionable and all. Kinda incident spook any person's future, most 'specially a child."

"Don't know 'bout it doin' any psycho damage, that's what you mean."

Betty stroked Miss Cutie's curls. There was not enough light in the room for Bet to see Cutie's hair.

"You know, Miss Pea, swear I *feel* the red. It travel from the innard and explode up hair."

" 'Member a fella, Cleon Tone, back in Arkansas, had him a congregation called the Church of the Fresh Start."

"That's good."

"Uh huh. Used to he'd say, 'Want you-all hand your-selfs a fresh start every day. Give everyone another chance."

"Sounds righteous enough," said Betty. "It hold up?"

Cutie giggled in the dark.

"He'da wished! Clean Cleon come asunder due to the dynamic charms of Aristidia Quenqui, wife of a deacon. Cleon Tone put the husband on his blankets-for-the-poor pickup run, durin' which time the mighty Reverend Clean served Mrs. Quenqui somethin' more'n another chance. Mr. Alford Quenqui come back kinda sudden one Saturday afternoon."

"Been a pretty sight."

"Usual thing, strangled 'em both. Last I knew Mr. Quenqui coolin' at the Federal Correctional Institute in Seagoville, Texas."

"Seems nothin' ends easy, Miss Pea."

"You really believe we can work a miracle with this colored man?"

"Rapture approachin', when the most faithful is instantly transformed into holy bodies and raised up to meet the Lord in the air. Be so much confusion after, Cutie, folks left searchin' for so many disappeared people. Mr. Lamar here either be skyborne or forgot."

"Then what, Bet?"

"Raptured holy brides of Miss Jesus, such as us, be rejoicin' seven years at the weddin' feast while the rest of the world, includin' them that's half-assed Christians, enters the Great Tribulation and most be slaughtered."

"How?"

" 'Lectrical storms, most likely, like that child on the beach at Waveland, Mississippi. The truly righteous be delivered but the unrepentant must perish. We be among the blameless, Miss Cutie. Not even one in ten be saved."

Cutie closed her eyes and whispered: "So because you are lukewarm, and neither hot nor cold, I will spit you out of My mouth."

Big Betty slid down and licked Cutie's erect left nipple.

DUKE'S SUITCASE

Vernon Duke Douglas could not expunge from his mind the image of the two decapitated Peruvian seamen. Duke, as he was called by his friends, was thirty-six years old and unmarried. He lived in a shotgun bungalow on Coffee Street in Chalmette, a blue-collar appendage to New Orleans, where he dined regularly at Rocky and Carlo's on St. Bernard Highway. He did his solitary drinking at Checkerboard Chucky's Change of Heart Bar in nearby Arabi, almost to Little Saigon.

When he was off-duty, Duke devoted most of his spare time to the study of astronomy, concentrating in particular on comets. It was his ambition to one day identify and have named after him a periodic comet, such as De Chéseaux's, Biela's, Di Vico's, Encke's, Donati's, Tuttle's, Coggia's, Swift's, d'Arrest's or the most famous of all, Halley's.

For a time, Duke was attracted primarily to minor planets—Ceres, Pallas, Juno, Vesta, Iris, Flora, Hygiea, Astraea, etc.—but became fascinated with Comet Schwassmann-Wachmann I when he learned that it had an orbit with an eccentricity so low that it could in fact be the orbit of a minor planet. Comets, of course, are at first sighting indistinguishable from minor planets, but between the orbits of Mars and Jupiter something strange occurs: the comet's shape appears less distinct, and then, nearer to Mars, the comet develops its tail.

It was Girolamo Fracastoro, one of Duke's heroes, along with Tycho Brahe and his collaborator, Johannes Kepler, the two men responsible for establishing the laws of planetary motion, who noticed that as a comet rounds the sun the tail points away from it, pushed ahead by radioactive pressure. At perihelion, nearest to the sun, the comet may lose its tail then grow another; and although the tail is clearly visible against the night sky, it is almost ephemeral. Duke was amazed to discover that if the tail of Halley's Comet could be compressed to the density of iron, it would fit into the smaller of his own two Samsonite suitcases.

The heads of Ernesto and Dagoberto Reyes, Duke thought, were like comets torn from their orbits, tails eviscerated. When he read in the *Times-Picayune* about a series of decapitations, all of males, having occurred along the western littoral of Florida, Duke decided to take his vacation time and pursue the phenomenon. That it could, in fact, be a non-periodic activity was possible, but his instinct, informed by a decade and a half of investigative work and observation, told him that however narrow or eccentric these ellipses might be, the connection to the cantalouped pair from Callao would prove valid.

During Roman times, Duke knew, people considered the appearance of a comet to be a bad omen, often blaming on it the subsequent loss of a battle. Duke also knew that he could not be the first to observe that the victors in the battle probably did not agree.

THE BEAST

"T he clouds here sure are beautiful."

"Always been the most special feature of Florida, sweet pea. Sunsets, especially."

"Sky looks different from an island, I think," Cutie said. "I mean, when you're on one. Even them jets streakin' over, like we just lost down here, part of what the world forgot."

Betty laughed and hugged her friend's shoulders.

"The world won't forget us, Miss Pea, providin' we leave 'em enough souvenirs, evidence of our sincerity."

"We gonna tattoo Mr. Lamar this mornin'?"

"What I figured to do. Mark him as he must be before beginnin' the lessons."

"And he causes all, the small and the great, and the rich and the poor, and the free man and the slaves, to be given a mark on their right hand or on the forehead."

Big Betty nodded and responded: "Here is wisdom. Let him who has understanding calculate the number of the beast, for the number is that of man; and his number is six hundred and sixty-six."

"As Miss Jesus is our witness," said Cutie, sparks coming from her big black eyes, "if anyone worships the beast and his image, and receives a mark on his forehead or upon his hand, he also will drink of the urine of the wrath of God, which is mixed in full-strength in the cup of Her anger; and he will be tormented with fire and brimstone in the presence of the holy angels—who is us—and in the presence of the Lamb."

As Cutie and Betty embraced, standing nude on the porch of the Trocadero Island Rod & Gun Club, a large nimbus cloud blocked the sun.

"And the smoke of their torment goes up forever and ever," said Betty; "and they have no rest day and night, those who worship the beast and his image, and whoever receives the mark of his name."

The women disengaged, stood back and regarded one another. Tears flowed simultaneously from their eyes.

"How we gonna do it?" asked Cutie.

"Straight razor. One I operated with on them sailors. Still plenty sharp."

"Head or hand?"

"Both. Mr. Lamar's smart. Could he'd cut off a spare appendage."

Cutie smiled and said, "You're smarter, Bet."

SNOWBALLS

How about that five-hundred-pound man got caught at the Miami airport attemptin' to smuggle more'n three hundred grams of crack cocaine under the tremendous folds of his stomach? Dogs sniffed out the dope—shepherds. Boy'll lose most that weight in prison, prob'ly be the second best thing coulda happened to him. Come out a new man."

Vernon Duke Douglas glanced at his Timex. Only twenty minutes until the plane would land at Tallahassee and he would not have to listen any longer to the woman seated next to him. She was about his own age, rail-thin, a brunette with green eyes and not entirely unattractive, but she had not stopped talking since before the aircraft had taken off from New Orleans. Her name was Petronia Weatherby, and she had introduced herself to Duke by saying, "I'll tell you my name, but you've got to promise not to ask, 'What will the weather be?' Or, 'What be the weather?' I hear it all the time." She had told Duke the purpose of her trip but he had already discharged the information from his memory bank.

"Conversation makes a flight go quicker, don't it, Mr. Douglas?" said Petronia. "You're not, now it occurs to ask, by any chance related to the movie-actin' Douglases, are you?"

"No, I'm not."

"Wouldn't I be somethin' lucky, you had. Couldn't control myself if I met someone really famous. I'd pee my pants in a whore's hurry, I know. I'm like that. Somethin' really wild happens? I just pee away. You know I ain't never seen snow, for example? Ice don't count; I mean real actual snow fall down. I ever do, I'll pee my pants. I'd die to throw a snowball, really I would."

"Comets are snowballs," said Duke.

"You mean those things shoot through the interplanetary air?"

Duke nodded. "They're composed of frozen gases, mostly carbon dioxide, methane or water vapor. Very little solid material. Their behavior is that of a ball of frozen gas being heated by the sun."

"I tell you, Mr. Douglas, I figured you for a scientific type right off, but now I see you're even a deeper person than most persons I've encountered on planes. Mind if I ask you a particularly scientific question?"

"Go ahead."

"Do women think different from men? I mean, their brain work another way? Technically speakin', that is."

Duke laughed. "I can't say, Ms. Weatherby. But I do know that dialogue between men and women seems to have about the consistency of a snowball. Some contain more ice than others, of course."

Petronia stared hard at Duke, her green eyes narrowing. He thought she was about to hiss.

"Now quick, before we land," she said, "I want to know the truth. Can there really be such a thing as a snowball in hell?"

PIGS

Mano and Boca Demente were as excited as the dogs. The cousins were less than a hundred yards from the sanitary landfill when Casanova, their catahoula, chased down a decent-sized boar, maybe three hundred-plus pounds of fighting pig, and had him backing up on a fifteen-foot-high mound of garbage. As soon as they reached the clearing, Boca released Diablo, their hundred-pound pit bull, who attacked instantly, catching the boar above the left shoulder. Diablo sank his incisors deep into the muscle and locked on while Casanova semicircled and barked, keeping the prey focussed. The infuriated boar could neither shake the pit nor reach him with his cutters, and with Diablo's weight attached had no chance of escaping the sleek catahoula.

Mano, unarmed, walked carefully around the snorting, frustrated swine, grabbed both hind legs and lifted them up about chest high. Boca came over, wrapped a thick length of nylon rope around the boar's legs, tied it off, then disengaged Diablo. As Mano dropped the pig, a chunk of fur and flesh shredded off its left shoulder. The boar rolled in the dirt, snorting and belching blood from its nostrils and mouth. Mano and Boca stood several paces away, holding the dogs with their left hands, high-fiveing each other with their right palms.

"*Un puerco grande, primo,* hey?" said Boca.

"Make a powerful mess of rib sandwiches, *seguro,*" said Mano.

The cousins, now both twenty-two years old, had been boar hunting without weapons, only dogs, since they were eighteen. They each stood six feet and weighed approximately two hundred pounds. Most people assumed they were brothers, since they resembled one another so closely, both having thick black hair, brown eyes and tan complexions. During the week, the Demente cousins operated their own house-painting business in Tallahassee, and on weekends they hunted pig for sport. Usually they hunted in Taylor County, around Perry, or further south, near Chiefland; but today they'd come to new territory, Trocadero Island, and not been disappointed.

The dogs were unmarked and Mano now took both of them back to the pickup, which was parked about a half-mile away. Boca removed his Bowie knife from its sheath, came around the squealing thing, tapping each tusk for luck with the tip of his knife as he did, and cut the rope. The pig leapt up and bounded into the woods.

Boca looked at the bloodstained ground and kicked dirt over it. He picked up the torn skin and chucked it into the bushes. This was a good spot for hunting and Boca did not want to leave any obvious evidence for the game warden. He re-sheathed his knife, picked up the pieces of rope and started toward the truck. He'd created an appetite and Boca assumed his cousin had one too.

THE BOOK OF BECOMING

"**D**rivin' down here, what kinda sign is that we seen?" Betty said to Rollo, whose hands and feet were bound by clothesline. He was seated in a chair. Betty and Cutie stood on either end of him, front and back.

"I don't know," said Rollo. "What sign?"

"One says, 'Have Some Tits with Your Grits.' Advert for a bare-ass place for truckers. Club G-String. Got a chain of these joints along the interstate. 'McSex,' I call 'em. That proper? That the way this country's supposed to go, you reckon?"

"Lots wrong with the country," said Rollo. "Most obscene of all is the lack of a national health program and dwindling funds for education. Just being alive a person is entitled to the best possible health care at no individual cost and a proper education. Anything less makes a travesty of the concept of civilization."

"Listen to him talk, Bet," Cutie said. "Sounds like a lawyer."

"I am a lawyer," said Rollo.

"Well, we're about to lay down the law to you, Mr. Lamar. Cutie, you can begin the first lesson now."

Cutie, who stood in front of Rollo, nodded and cleared her throat. She held in her hands a large, peach-colored loose-leaf notebook.

"This here's the *Book of Becoming*," she said, "the only one in existence, and we got it. Which, of course, is no mystery how that is since it was me and Bet who wrote it. We done it while we was in prison. Written between the lines of letters we got had already been censored, so we could take 'em out with us."

"*Still* writin' it," said Big Betty.

"More parts to come, most certainly."

"From the beginnin'," Betty instructed.

Cutie read aloud:

THE BOOK OF BECOMING

Lesson One

EVERYBODY is a **SINNER**. If not for the eternal presence of Miss Jesus our Holy Mother and One True Companion we the Ordinary and mostly futile failures would never be gived a Second Chance. The Female Side is about to Explode and Destroy the Male who done most everything wrong from the Beginning. It is the Male who made the Planet dirty and devoured the Female Soul.

Now we shall witness the Resurrection of the Female Soul so the Planet might could be Saved. So saith us Disciples of Miss Jesus.

We are approaching the Last Days unless this Warning is heeded. The Beast of Revelations shall stalk forth on his hind legs and mash Believers and Unbelievers alike on his path. SINNERS must become BELIEVERS and the Male Evildoers make way for the Female Side or there shall be NO HOPE.

As foretold by Matthew who was a Gay Male there will be a real Tribulation such as has not occurred since the beginning of the World until now nor ever shall. This Tribulation shall befall the Male Side who is by Nature the Unbelievers despite their Lies and shall beset them with the most undescribable form of Human Destruction ever in Human History. As set forth in Revelations it shall be unimaginable Pain and Suffering for the Unbelievers. The sun will be dark and the moon become like blood. Following this shall be wars and big earthquakes and plagues and hail and fire mixed with blood burning half the Earth. So shall mountains and islands be rent from their original place and seas become blood and water too bitter to drink. The Male Unbelievers shall thirst to death and there will be but the Female Side to greet Miss Jesus.

The Triumph of the Female Believers is evident in their survival. Miss Jesus shall extend Her Hand to them that are liberated forever from control of the Unholy Male name of Satan. Only a Single Male reborn with an entire Reformed Attitude may attend the Female Formation of

the New World according to Miss Jesus. This witness shall gather proof and Die Blessed.

Amen.

"Amen," said Betty. "You gettin' the picture, Mr. Lamar?"

He nodded. "I got the negative."

ONE MORE FOR THE ROAD

Vernon Duke Douglas rented a Mercury Cougar at the Tallahassee airport and headed for the Gulf Coast. He stopped in Sopchoppy at the Love Nest Cafe for a hamburger and a Dr Pepper, then drove to Apalachicola, where he stayed overnight at the Gorrie Inn, named for John Gorrie, inventor of the ice machine. The next morning Duke was up early, drawing a bead on Egypt City, where he figured to pick up a lead.

As he drove, the scenery reminded Duke of the time he'd helped pull four bodies from the swamp at Irish Bayou. A Cambodian refugee had gone down to fish near the unfinished castle and hooked a right hand with his ten-pound test line. The Cambo brought the hand, which was missing the pinkie, to a Viet restaurant near Arabi, and asked a waitress if they could cook it up for him.

The restaurant owner called the police, who came right over and made the Cambo take them to the place where he'd found the hand.

Duke, who was working on a missing persons case, was notified, and he met them at Irish Bayou. It took no more than forty minutes of dragging that stretch before four bloated corpses surfaced. None of the bodies, all males, was missing a right hand, but each had been decapitated, probably by a broken-toothed handsaw, given the irregular pattern to the cuts. The heads were never found, and the person for whom Duke had been searching was not among them. The Cambo, Duke recalled, had asked if he could keep the hand.

In Egypt City, Duke checked into the Hernando Cortés Motor Court, a place that no doubt had been a popular winter retreat for snowbirds during the 1940s and '50s, but was now the target site for a new mall. It was cheap, though, which was all Duke Douglas cared about, a place to flop. It was eight o'clock when he walked sixty paces down the shell pathway to a little restaurant called The Polynesia that the old guy motel clerk had said made a more than decent conch chowder.

"You sleep alone, too?"

Duke looked up from his bowl of chowder to a woman who had slid into the booth on the seat opposite his. She was about thirty, an overweight brunette with a pretty, Indian-looking face and large breasts.

"Too?" he said.

"You're eatin' alone, ain't ya?"

"I was."

"Well, just askin'. Mind if I smoke?"

Before Duke could answer, she lit up a Viceroy, took a deep puff and exhaled away from him.

"This restaurant is one hundred percent smoking area," she said. "See the sign on the door?"

"Didn't notice."

"You don't smoke, do ya?"

"No."

"You screw?"

"Lady, do you own this place?"

"Uh uh. Never been in before. I'm just a big girl on the road."

"Then why don't you sit someplace else while I eat my dinner."

"For twenty bucks I'll fuck your brains out, mister. Hell, for fifty you can have me all night, do me up the heinie, you prefer. Lots of boys been on low-payin' state holidays find it suits 'em now. I got two awesome wombos you can hang from like a monkey, case you ain't paid attention."

The woman smiled at Duke, showing a full complement of even, tobacco-stained teeth. Duke had to admit to himself that she was not altogether unattractive.

"What's your name?" he asked.

"Wapiti Touché. I'm Seminole-Irish on my mama's side, French Canadian and Danish on my daddy's. You interested in genealogy? I'm writin' a book on the history of the Great Red Kings of Ireland."

Wapiti Touché took a sharp drag on her Viceroy. "Finish your soup, honey, it's goin' cold."

Duke bent to it, not unamused by this strange person.

"Better with Tabasco, don't you think?" she said. "Always put in lots of Saltine crumbles, lime juice and hot sauce so my nose runs. Can't help it, that's the way I like it. So, you and me gonna do the time? Forty, all night or you had enough."

Wapiti lifted her shoeless left foot up under the table and planted it gently in Duke's crotch. She massaged his penis with her toes and felt it stir.

"Y'all are sure responsive," she said, smiling again.

"Let's start with twenty," said Duke.

As soon as they were in Duke's room at the Hernando Cortés Motor Court, Wapiti told him she needed a few moments of privacy and quickly disappeared into the bathroom. Duke sat down in the only chair and unlaced his shoes, surprised that he should so be looking forward to fucking this two-hundred-pound part-Indian woman. He heard the toilet flush and pulled off his shoes and socks, stood up and undid his belt. Wapiti Touché appeared stark naked and jumped on to the bed, her huge breasts ricocheting against her chest like fully inflated volleyballs bouncing off a hardwood floor. She reached over and unzipped Duke's pants, pulled them down and dragged him under her. His cock was already hard and she straddled him, hammering his cheeks with her tits.

Duke was dazed, and before he realized what was happening, he felt himself about to come.

"Wapiti, wait!" he shouted. "Not so fast!"

Wapiti put a pillow over Duke's face and shut him up. She was extremely strong and outweighed him by twenty-five pounds. Wapiti felt Duke's cock jerk twice, and then he was dead.

A WOMAN'S TOUCH

Rollo decided he would fake a heart attack. If the women bought it, Rollo thought, then either they would abandon him or drop him at a hospital. It was definitely worth a shot. He'd do it during the next lesson, when Cutie started in on that "Miss Jesus Says" routine. Rollo really did not want to suffer it anymore. He was lying in his sleeping bag just before dawn, thinking this, when he heard the motorcycles slide to a stop outside.

"Shit, Bet, what's that?" asked Cutie.

"Sounds like choppers."

Big Betty leapt up, pulled on her clothes and picked up her gun.

"C'mon, Cutie. Some boys is sure to be surprised."

Jump Start and Badger, members of the Lucky Dogs M.C. from Bon Secour, Alabama, each lifted a second leg off their hogs and stood and stretched as the planet tipped over and light leaked in. On the backs of their jean jackets, within the horseshoed letters advertising their vehicular and geographical affiliation, was a silk-screened drawing of a mastiff holding a bloody, severed hand in its jaws.

"Looks like a proper place to crash, Badg, what you think?"

Badger rubbed the grime-encrusted palm of his right hand over his six-day beard, rubbed his chest across the words BILLY'S SEAFOOD COUNTY ROAD 10 WEST on his T-shirt, scratched the crown of his greasy, shoulder-length-brown-haired head, and yawned. He looked over at Jump Start, who, but for a cherry-red glass left eye and no left ear, could have been his twin. Both Jump Start's eye and ear had been torn from their rightful places during a bar fight in Town 'n' Country, outside Tampa, one Saturday night several years before. Jump could hardly remember what life had been like before he'd lost those items.

He did think every now and then, however, about three-hundred-pound Bevo Rubber, the since-deceased old boy who had done him this harm. After Jump had gotten out of the hospital, he and Badger had paid a very early morning visit to Bevo Rubber's trailer and hacked off both of his hands with machetes before Bevo could fingerprint the sawed-off Mossberg twelve-gauge he kept under his pillow. Then, while Badger held down the flabbergasted Rubber, Jump Start had used his pocket-pack Trim tweezers on the bovine's eyes. They left Bevo Rubber alone and screaming inside his tin-can domicile, the door of which Badger blocked while Jump Start lit a fuse stuck in a porto-tank of propane and rolled it underneath the trailer. The Lucky Dogs were on their hogs and gone when the Airstream went up, probably taking a couple of Bevo's slumbering neighbors along with him to white trash hell.

"Could use a rest, J.S.," Badger said. "This ol' meetin' lodge looks about abandoned."

Inside the Trocadero Island Rod & Gun Club, Big Betty and Miss Cutie waited patiently for the intruders. Cutie had placed a wide strip of duct tape across Rollo's mouth and he lay motionless, his hands and feet securely bound by clothesline. Jump Start opened the door and Betty shot him point blank in his glass eye.

"Damn!" shouted Badger, as he hit the ground and rolled out of the shooter's sight.

He ran for his Harley, kicked it to life, and roared off onto the highway, where he was immediately broadsided by a fully restored 1956 Ford pickup with two men in the cab and two dogs riding in the bed. Badger went down and the truck braked to a stop, at which point the dogs leaped out and attacked the fallen biker. Before either of the crash-shocked Demente cousins could pull Diablo away, the enraged pit had bitten Badger to death. Mano Demente held Diablo by the collar while his cousin, Boca, took off after Casanova, the catahoula, who was freaked-out, yelping and screeching as he zigzagged along the blacktop.

A couple of moments later, Betty and Cutie fishtailed onto the state road in their black Monaco. Mano jumped out of the way without letting go of Diablo, and watched helplessly as the careening Dodge barely avoided Boca but clipped Casanova, sending the hound sprawling, its right foreleg fractured.

As Big Betty blasted onto the bridge, raced through the stoplight at the junction with the interstate and headed the Dodge in the direction of Pensacola, the highway patrol car parked on the shoulder of the road in front of Jasper Pasco's Fishin' Pier and Grocery sparked up and went after her, siren on and spirals pulsing.

"Why you didn't plug Mr. Lamar, Bet?" Cutie asked. "He'll be able to identify us."

"Seemed like he was takin' the teachin's to heart, sweet pea, you know?"

Betty laughed, glanced in the rearview mirror and eyeballed the beige-and-white hot on their tail.

"Kiddin', Cutie," she said, looking ahead again. "Forgot about him in the excitement, is all. Don't make no difference. As Miss Jesus is our Guide, before this shootin' match is over every man'll know a woman's touch."

MIDNIGHT EVERYWHERE

Easy Earl drove the Mercury Monarch slowly, no more than twenty miles per hour, along St. Claude Avenue in New Orleans. It was eleven fifty-eight P.M., almost Wednesday, raining again. Thunderstorms day and night, lately. Earl switched on his wipers. The personalized license plates on his fire engine red 1978 Merc read EZY EARL, not EASY because there could be only seven figures, not eight, but it was good enough for Earl, whose last name was Blakey, like the great jazz drummer's. Earl, who was forty-six years old and never married, was headed from his house on St. Roch to his job at the post office on Camp Street, where he worked as a truck loader. His shift began at midnight and he knew he would be a little late, but he could blame the rain.

The car radio was tuned to WWOZ. Sam Cooke and

the Soul Stirrers were singing "That's Heaven to Me."
Terrible about Sam Cooke gettin' taken out like he did,
thought Earl. Shot down by a old lady in a motel.
Woman claimed he been abusin' a girl. Man sure did
have a beautiful voice.

The record ended and the deejay said: "It's a new day
in the Crescent City. From Florida comes news of two
women being held on suspicion of a series of murders, all
of men, dating back to last year. Bettina Stalcup and
Carol Early were taken into custody today in Pensacola
on murder charges ranging across the states of Florida,
Alabama and Louisiana. Authorities say the women,
both ex-convicts, claim to be brides of Jesus, whom the
suspects insist was also a woman. 'Miss Jesus,' they say,
ordered them to rid the world of the male species. 'Men
is beyond the point of being reeducated. The disease has
spread too far,' said Ms. Stalcup. 'It is midnight everywhere for them.'"

Easy Earl shook his head, pulled a Kool from his shirt
pocket, stuck it between his lips and punched in the
dashboard lighter.

"Mm, mm," he mumbled, "sure as shit some righteous
bitches out there."

2

THE SECRET LIFE OF INSECTS

Estranged from beauty none can be
For beauty is infinity,
And power to be finite ceased
When fate incorporated us.

—Emily Dickinson

BEATIFICA

No way God meant a woman shouldn't have control over her own body," said Beatifica Brown to Easy Earl Blakey as they sat on adjoining stools at the High Heaven Bar on Burgundy Street in New Orleans's Eighth Ward.

Beatifica Brown, born in La Ceiba, República de Honduras, had emigrated to Tampa, Florida, at the age of three with her parents, Fábula and German Moreno. Beatifica had anglicized her surname during her tenure as a detainee in the Fort Sumatra Detention Center for Wayward Women, six years before, on her thirtieth birthday, May 9, a date she shared with her hero, the Kansas abolitionist John Brown.

As John Brown's cause was freedom from slavery, Beatifica's mission was freedom of choice. She was an abortionist, though never trained as a medical doctor, and she had done time for performing illegal operations in Florida. Beatifica had come to New Orleans after the Louisiana State Legislature had enacted the most repressive anti-abortion law in the country. Her intent was to practice what she considered to be her calling, and spread the gospel of a woman's right to choose.

"I'm goin' to spit in the eye of the demon," Beatifica Brown said to her fellow inmates, Big Betty Stalcup and Miss Cutie Early, a few days prior to her release from Fort Sumatra. Betty and Cutie, who had devised an agenda based on a self-contained philosophy of their own, had blessed Beatifica, and told her to always remember Miss Jesus was walking with her every step of the way.

Miss Jesus notwithstanding, Beatifica had developed her plan based on her own experience, having been rendered incapable of further child-bearing as a result of a botched abortion performed on her when she was sixteen. Beatifica had been impregnated by a boy named Delbert Bork, a high school classmate. It was Delbert who took Beatifica to the trailer of a man claiming to be a doctor, they paid him $150, and he ruined her for life. Since that time, Beatifica had taken up the sword, determined that other women with unwanted pregnancies should not have to suffer as she had.

Beatifica had found a woman named Basenji Jones, a registered nurse in Tampa, who believed as she did, and who taught Beatifica the proper procedure for abortion. Basenji also introduced Beatifica to the freedom-of-choice underground of the Deep South, in whose fundamentalist-crazed atmosphere abortion was considered a practice no less heinous than miscegenation. German and Fábula, being Catholics, recoiled in horror when their daughter told them of her mission, but they were powerless in the face of her zeal.

"Woman got to do what she need, I agree," said Earl, lifting a Crown Royal and milk on the rocks to his lips. "Fact is, Miz Brown, reason I wanted to talk to you is my lady, Rita. She already got four children and don't be needin' another."

"How far along is she?"

"Two, two-and-a-half months, she figure. I got me a good job at the post office, Miz Brown. Be glad to pay however much."

"I don't take for myself, Earl, only for the cause. The price is whatever you can afford."

Easy Earl swallowed the rest of his drink. Somebody punched up Percy Sledge proselytizing on "When a Man Loves a Woman" on the giant old Rock-Ola underneath the 3' x 4' reproduction of Cézanne's *Une moderne Olympia*.

"You most definitely is a godsend, Miz Brown," said the relieved Earl.

Beatifica picked up her glass of straight Tanqueray with a teaspoonful of sugar in it and saluted him.

"Never doubt myself for a minute, Mr. Blakey. Keep the faith," she said, and drained it.

JOHN BROWN'S WISH

Beatifica had first heard the song about John Brown when she was a child, but the lyrics meant nothing to her until she found her vocation. Many times each day Beatifica sang to herself, *"John Brown's body lies a-mouldering in the grave."* She kept among her few belongings F. B. Sanborn's book *Life and Letters of John Brown,* published in 1885, and had been for eight years making notes toward the composition of a monograph entitled *John Brown and the Divine Notion.* Beatifica's treatise was based on Wendell Phillips's identification of "letters of marque from God" as the foundation of John Brown's conviction that he was entitled to destroy slavery by violent means.

John Brown, a descendant of *Mayflower* Puritans, had been born in Connecticut and raised in Ohio, and at the age of forty-nine he moved to the state of New York, where he farmed land contiguous to that worked by black settlers. He had already made plain his hatred of slavery, and soon thereafter John Brown joined five of his sons in Kansas, the border state from which he launched his active campaign of opposition to the odious institution. Following bloody confrontations with pro-slavers in Kansas, John Brown led his followers to Canada, Massachusetts and finally to Virginia, where his plan was to establish a stronghold in which fugitive slaves could take refuge.

On the night of October 16, 1859, with only eighteen men, five of whom were Negro slaves, John Brown led an attack on a federal arsenal at Harpers Ferry. They captured the arsenal and took as hostages sixty of the town's leading citizens. The next two days saw the abolitionists laid siege to by a force of United States Marines, led by Colonel Robert E. Lee. The Marines ultimately overpowered the free-staters, killing ten of them, including two of John Brown's sons. Brown was captured, being seriously wounded after his surrender. Within the month he had been tried and found guilty of "treason, and conspiring and advising with slaves and other rebels, and murder in the first degree." On December 2, he was hanged. John Brown had fathered twenty children by two wives.

Beatifica felt a powerful connection to her nineteenth-century namesake, and was convinced that she also carried "letters of marque from God." Like John Brown, Beatifica had identified her immediate enemies, among whom was a militant pro-life New Orleans preacher named Dallas Salt, pastor of the non-sectarian

Church on the One Hand, located on Elysian Fields Avenue. Dallas Salt's sister, Dilys, was an equally militant pro-choice preacher who had broken with Dallas over the abortion issue, and established her own ministry, the Church on the Other Hand, directly across the street from her brother's. Each Sunday, the Salt siblings exhorted their respective flocks to study against the opposition.

Beatifica had attended both congregations: Brother Dallas's Church on the One Hand in order to know her enemy at close quarters; and Sister Dilys's Church on the Other Hand to lend her support. It was Brother Dallas, of course, who had the larger ministry, and who was allowed access to the airwaves, broadcasting for an hour on radio station WGOD at midnight Sundays. The Church on the Other Hand was constantly under siege, its building regularly vandalized and its members, most of whom were women, threatened and terrorized. Sister Dilys was never left unguarded, her constant companions being several of the most rugged members of the Sisters of Clytemnestra Motorcycle Club.

Beatifica Brown knew that to be successful in her role she had to maintain a low profile, to carry out her mission with a minimum of attention. She was content to let others, such as Dilys Salt, carry on the fight in a public fashion, while she made her services available to all who were in need and proselytized as occasions arose.

On one wall of her room on Decatur Street, at the edge of the Quarter near Esplanade, Beatifica had hung a framed photograph of John Brown, his wild eyes burning in his bearded face. Across the bottom of her hero's

picture she had written, "His Soul Goes Marching On."
Beatifica knew it was she, the Unknown Warrior, who
would assassinate Dallas Salt when John Brown spoke
to her as she slept on her ninth night in New Orleans,
their common number. Beatifica awoke, sat up in bed,
shook her shoulder-length red hair, felt the length of her
body shudder, nodded her head numerous times and said
aloud, "Yes, yes, it is my wish also!"

THE REWARD

Dilys Salt stood at the bedroom window of her second-story apartment on Pauger Street, staring at the group of ten or more people carrying signs and walking back and forth on the sidewalk below. Some of the signs said: **KILL THE MESSENGER, NOT THE FETUS; LIFE IS TOO GOOD FOR SISTER DILYS; THE OTHER HAND MUST BE BANNED;** and **BABIES CRY: DON'T KILL US, DILYS!** "They out there again?" asked Terry Perez, one of the Sisters of Clytemnestra and Dilys's current lover.

"Every day now," said Dilys. "Cops can't do nothin' about it, they say, long as the demonstrators stick to the other side of the street. Free speech. Hah! Fools don't recognize a woman's right to govern her own self, but they do allow a body to be harassed on her home ground."

"I could call some of the Sisters, have 'em ride their bikes into the crowd."

"Bad idea, Terry. Girls'd get run in and I'd be blamed. Best to leave 'em be. Get used to it and carry on."

Dilys lit a cigarette and sat down in a wicker chair. She was nude except for her red panties and Terry's black Chippewa motorcycle boots. She crossed her legs and smoked. Terry was sitting on the bed, wearing only her sleeveless club jacket, brushing out her long black hair. She and Dilys had been lovers for a month now, the longest, Terry knew, that Dilys ever had been exclusively with one of Clytemnestra's members.

"What you thinkin' 'bout, Dilys?"

"Oh, my daughter, I guess."

"You got a daughter? I didn't know that."

Dilys took a deep drag on her Pall Mall and exhaled a snake's length of smoke.

"She's fourteen tomorrow, one November. Had her when I was twenty-six."

"What's her name?"

"Pillara. Her daddy chose it."

"Where is she?"

"She got the Down's syndrome, used to be was called mongoloid, 'cause of the facial features. I keep her in a home in Plain Dealin', near where my mama moved to after Daddy died."

"Where was it you was raised?"

"Queen City, Texas. Mama moved over by Plain Dealin' to be near her people up in Ida. Made sense to put Pillara in a place close where Mama can look in on her, see she's bein' treated right."

"You don't visit her, huh?"

"Not in twelve years. Pillara ain't never really known me."

"How 'bout her daddy? He go see her?"

Dilys gave a short, cruel laugh. "He seen her once only. Saw she was deformed, named her and left the rest to me."

"You and him ain't in touch, I take it."

"Oh, yeah, we ain't never been out of touch. Terry, I like you a lot, you know. More'n almost anyone I been with in a very long time. If you promise not to tell anybody else, I'll let you in on a almost-secret."

Terry stopped brushing her hair and looked at Dilys, whose cobalt blue eyes bored into her.

"I promise," Terry whispered.

"Dallas Salt is Pillara's daddy."

Terry dropped her brush.

"But he's your brother!"

Dilys nodded. " 'Incest is best,' what he used to say."

"I gotta pee," said Terry, as she hopped off the bed and ran to the toilet.

Dilys sucked hard on her cigarette, then stubbed it out on the heel of Terry's left boot. She flicked the butt away and spread her legs as Terry reentered the room.

"Honey?" said Dilys, sliding her panties off. "Come kneel near the source and taste of its fruit."

"Oh, Dilys," said Terry, dropping down, "you got the most pain!"

Dilys closed her eyes as Terry bent to it, eliciting a deep groan from her supine pastor.

"Pain is temporal, Terry," Dilys said, stroking her lover's sleek hair with her right hand. "Pleasures such as these serve to remind us of our reward, which is to come."

LIGHT-YEARS FROM HOME

At forty-six years old, Dallas Salt, all six-foot-six, two hundred fifty-five pounds of him, had never before been as confident in himself and what he was doing as he was now. He still had a full head of hair, which he had dyed black once a month, and he worked out daily for at least an hour on the Universal gym equipment in the basement of the church building. Never married, Dallas Salt maintained an active sex life, his taste running these days to heavily prophylacticized anal sex with skinny black hookers procured for him by Sabine Yama, his half-Cajun, half-Pakistani aide-de-camp for the last fifteen years. Many of these women had become members of Dallas Salt's flock, a fact that delighted him, though once they accepted his sermon, Dallas told Sabine, he would not allow them to accept his semen.

The Church on the One Hand was flourishing since the step-up in anti-abortion action. Attendance for the Sunday services was at capacity, and the television ministry was expanding rapidly. Fifty-six cable outlets across the South now carried Brother Dallas's messages. His sister's ministry provided fuel for his fire. Dallas loved Dilys dearly, he always had, and he had no private objection to her preaching. Dallas did worry about Dilys's welfare, however, and instructed Sabine Yama to keep a close watch on their own most fervent followers, those most likely to attempt to physically harm her. Only Sabine, among Dallas's inner circle, knew of the existence of Pillara Salt, and that Dilys was the girl's mother.

Sabine, who was five-foot-five, fat and mostly bald, had a club left foot and a withered right arm due to birth defects. He was more than a little bit in love with Brother Dallas, a fact of which Pastor Salt was well aware, and of which he took full advantage, keeping Sabine on call on virtually a round-the-clock basis. Now thirty-two, Sabine had fallen under the influence of the Salts when he was barely into his teens, his parents having been horrified by their grotesque of an only son, who, moreover, exhibited unnatural proclivities beginning at the age of ten, when Sabine began tricking tourists on Bourbon Street. He went to work for the Salts, who saw in him the virtue of loyalty to those willing to offer a helping hand.

When the break occurred, Sabine opted to remain with Dallas, mostly because of his preference for male company, and knowing that his role in Dilys's circle, despite her genuine affection for him, would be of a secondary nature. Sabine hated the Sisters of Clytemnestra, who, he felt, were an unfortunate influence on Dilys, pushing her further from her avowed purpose in life, which was to help people come to know their truest self, the inner being belonging to God.

This abortion issue, Sabine believed, had been blown all out of proportion. He could not deny the fact that there were an awful lot of loose canons on the streets the world would doubtless be better off without, but he once had been among the unwanted himself, light-years from home, and Sabine never lost sight of that reality. Dallas said there were perhaps two million abortions performed, legally and illegally, every year in the United States alone. Those souls, Sabine knew, were recycled throughout the universe, safe on other planets if not on Earth. Sabine often wondered if he would not have been better off inhabiting, say, a Martian form, and, of course, what his penis would be like.

THE RIGHT CHOICE

Beatifica entered Elvis Steck's Super Surplus Store on lower Magazine and was immediately approached by a pink-faced person who looked to be in his early thirties. The man was about six feet tall and had to weigh, Beatifica guessed, no less than three hundred pounds. He wore green-tinted magnifying glasses with adjustable double lenses, a red Yosemite Sam mustache, and what appeared to be a navy blue rubber leisure suit surrounded by a stretch-nylon Sam Browne holster belt. Beatifica could not help but notice the brown handle of a revolver conveniently placed at right-front crotch level, the Hurricane holster unstrapped.

"Afnoon, mame," the giant man said. "Evis Steck, soiv an protec. Ken Ah hep you wit?"

"Need somethin' to shoot with, Mr. Steck. Somethin'

other than uses bullets but stop a bull, I wanted."

Elvis Steck smiled, showing his front teeth, one of which was a cap with the head of an American bald eagle on it.

"Got da ting. Ovuh cheer."

Beatifica followed the human mountain to a side counter, which Elvis Steck somehow managed to squeeze behind. He took a box from a shelf, opened it and set the contents in front of them.

"Dis cheer's branoo. Stealth Airrow Gun. Woik unna wattuh, dass way de bull go. Ha teck ah gun system, put enny ahchry quip out uh biz. Propel ba compress ayuh, dass CO^2. Arras shoot twicet fass standid crossbows, tree-sixt eff pee ess upt fahv-hund eff pee ess ba ya re-moof de reggalate, wit twicet foot pown uv impac. Free floatin bell low fa pin-pawn acksee fum fawt trew hun-net yawds. Manwill top triggaz full adjustbill faw tot-ness, travel an faw numba shots fum de powuh sauce. Wat proof, lak Ah say, funkshnull buv aw below de wattuh. Ahcraf loomnum an stainless steel with a bead-blastid, anodaz black finish. Sixteen-inch bell assembly, brawdhead gawd, clapsbill stawk, wun pawnt fahv-fahv ba twenny millimeetuh zoom scope, rings, empty seven-ounce refillbill cylinduh wit valve, six sixteen-inch loomnum arras an a eighteen na haf ba fawteen ba fahv na haf wattuhproof case. Whole packich weigh faw pown, tree ounce. Brawdhead hunt tips extra."

"How much?"

"Wit aw witout extra bladetips?"

"Without. Six should be enough."

"Fifteen-hunnet."

"I'll take it."

"Chawge?"

"Cash."

"Ony way da go. You made da rat choss."

Elvis Steck packed the Airrow Gun in the box and Beatifica laid fifteen new hundred-dollar bills on the counter. She looked up and read a sign posted on the wall.

IF THEY MOVE,
SHOOT 'EM.

MAGNOLIAS

hat can I do you
for, Miss?"

Beatifica sat at the counter of the Choctaw Cafe on
Iberville Street, checking out the menu. She looked up
into the ugliest face she had ever seen and shuddered
violently, as if in a dream she had been suddenly embraced by a cadaver and could not pry apart from her
body its stiff, icy arms.

"I ask, can I get you somethin', or you need more
time?"

Beatifica forced herself to look again at the man. His
face was completely purple, the skin covered by a birth-
mark that reached halfway down the man's neck. Inside
the epidermal mask his eyes shimmered like gas lan-
terns on a moonless night.

"Just coffee," Beatifica said, resisting the urge to bolt
out of the place.

A few stools away, a small, pudgy, completely bald-headed man, wearing a dirty white T-shirt, red suspenders and yellow Bermuda shorts, who could have been anywhere from seventy to ninety years old, was talking to the counterman in a rapid, raspy growl.

"I put Kid Magnolia against Basilio in Chi. Tore him right up. Ya shoulda seen it. Basilio couldn't read the big E for weeks. Then the Kid gets married. This devil bitch tore his guts out like Tiger Flowers couldn't. Like Sandy Saddler couldn't. Like Gavilan or Pep or Griffith in his prime, when he wasn't makin' hats. Nobody. She took all the dough I'd saved for him and spread it from Canal Street to Michigan Avenue. When she was ready for the big time, she pushed him into the Garden with Sugar.

"I wanted him to go in with LaMotta, who he could have run and cut for twelve till they stopped it. LaMotta was an animal, he wouldn't go down, and a much better boxer than he's given credit for, but the Kid would've cut him to pieces. We couldn't get the kind of money his saint of a life's companion needed from LaMotta, so we made the date with Sugar. It lasted five. Ray had the Kid down three times before that. He wasn't ready, wasn't up for it. She used that pussy of hers so he wouldn't listen to me, Joey Falco, nobody.

"Of course she left him. Took up with a pimp in Camden, or God knows. But the Kid was finished. He had no confidence left and couldn't get it back. Couldn't pay for it. Got him in with Dynamite Daley when Daley was on the needle and the Kid lasted six. Six! With a junkie! Got him Virgil Akins and he went two. Last time was with Giardello in Jersey and it was over before Falco could take the stool out of the ring.

"He ended nowhere, like King Levinsky, who wound up peddlin' handpainted ties around swimmin' pools in Miami. That wife of his made him too mother-jumpin' *certain,* and that's no good. That's when things tend to slip away."

Beatifica put a dollar on the counter and left without touching her coffee.

VICTIMS OF RECEIVED INFORMATION

Sister Dilys Salt stood at the podium in the Church on the Other Hand and surveyed her congregation. All 401 seats were occupied and another 100 people or so were wedged in around the sides and at the rear of the room. Loudspeakers had been set up outside to carry Sister Dilys's sermon to those forced by order of the Orleans Parish Fire Department to remain on the church steps, at the foot of which were gathered approximately fifty protestors, anti-abortion activists who were present whenever Dilys spoke. A line of beefy Sisters of Clytemnestra insured that the demonstrators would not attempt to invade the premises, as they had done in the past.

"Sisters united!" Dilys began, as she always did. "And you all-too-few brothers in arms, welcome to the Church on the Other Hand. A warning to those of you out there who oppose us: Do not confuse body parts, namely hand with cheek. We will not turn or be turned! The neverending plague of ignorance is carried by victims of received information, unfortunates fallen prey to the Fear Riders. Be advised: The enlightened adherents to the beliefs of the Church on the Other Hand will not be trampled! We stand firm on the higher ground of free choice. There shall be no retreat to the shadows. No longer will it be our blood displayed on the swordblade! The One Hand falls as the Other Hand is raised! Then shall we say also unto them on the one hand, Depart from me, ye cursed, into everlasting fire, prepared for the devil and his angels."

While Dilys Salt's flock rocked to her pronouncements, Dallas Salt sat in his dressing room across the street, his eyes closed, as Fatima Verdad, a fifteen-year-old prostitute whom Sabine Yama had driven over from Algiers, stood behind him, massaging the preacher's ears and the back of his neck with her milk chocolate breasts while he masturbated. Fatima Verdad was extremely thin, in accordance with Dallas's preference, so her relatively large breasts were a bonus so far as he was concerned. Dallas pulled lazily at his semi-erect cock, completely relaxed, listening to Fatima hum.

"What's that tune, honey?" he asked.

"Wan' I stop?"

"No, no, baby. I like it. You know the name?"

"Be 'Things That Make You Go Hmmmm' by C & C Music Fact'ry."

"You sure do make me go hm-m. Lean over more, precious, put your sweet tits 'gainst my cheeks."

"I gon' be a singer, too," Fatima Verdad said, as she stood on her toes and lifted her breasts in her hands and rubbed the nipples on Dallas Salt's face. "A real one, though, not like some girl only dance an' preten' to sing."

The preacher stroked himself faster.

"I dance good as Paula Abdul, too. You like Paula Abdul? She cute but ain' got no tiddies."

"Come around now, baby," said Dallas. "Move quick, girl!"

Fatima, who was entirely naked except for a black velvet choker with a pearl cross on it that Sabine Yama had made her put on before bringing her in, knelt in front of Dallas Salt, as Sabine had instructed her to do when explaining the pastor's needs, and blew gently on the head of his penis as it grew fat and red. The prostitute kept her face still while Dallas Salt's semen pelted it, not flinching even when some flew into her left eye. After he had finished, the preacher rested for a few moments with his eyes shut, still holding his shrinking prick.

"You done fine, girl," he said, finally, looking at Fatima Verdad. "Sabine!" he shouted.

Sabine Yama came in from just outside the door, where he had been waiting.

"Show her where to clean up and give her some extra taxi money. How much time I got till the broadcast?"

"About fifteen minutes."

Sabine handed him a towel, which Dallas used to wipe off his hand and leg.

"Whew! Used to it didn't take so long gettin' primed," said Dallas, standing up.

He watched Fatima Verdad as she stepped into her panties.

"Bless you, honey," Dallas said. "Hope to hear you on the radio one of these days pretty soon."

Fatima smiled, showing big white teeth. "Be doin' it, with God's help."

Dallas nodded, and said, "Baby, He might could do worse."

NIGHTCAP AT RUBY'S

CARIBBEAN

"**S**abine, darlin', one more of these and I'll even go to bed with you!"

Jimmy Sermo and Sabine Yama were at Ruby's Caribbean Bar on Poland Avenue, drinking Bombay and listening to the jukebox. Little Johnny Taylor had just now wailed on "Love Bones" and Fabrice Dos Veces, the transsexual Cuban bartender, offered a free drink to whoever would play "Lookin' for a Love" by The Valentinos. Sabine hopped down from his stool, limped over, pushed a few quarters into the Rock-Ola, and punched up Fabrice's request, along with "The Things That I Used to Do" by Guitar Slim and "Nite Owl" by Tony Allen and the Champs. By the time Sabine had climbed back onto his stool, there was a fresh Bombay on the rocks with a twist of lime waiting for him.

"*Gracias*, Sabine," said Fabrice, as Bobby Womack's sweaty voice surged into the room.

Jimmy Sermo slid off of his stool onto the floor and stayed there, curled up in a fetal position on the brown-and-white tiles. He was a short, thin man of thirty-one, with wavy blonde hair and hazel eyes that, due to his alcoholism, were bloodshot most of the time. Jimmy and Sabine had known each other since both had been child prostitutes, and they met occasionally at Ruby's Caribbean or the Saturn for drinks. Jimmy now worked in a laundromat on St. Ann, his once angelic looks having deteriorated badly over the years. His disheveled and dissolute appearance disturbed Sabine, who had tried unsuccessfully to get Jimmy to seek the counsel of Dallas Salt.

The last time Sabine had suggested it, Jimmy Sermo said, "That faggot's your savior, not mine."

"Brother Dallas ain't a faggot," Sabine replied.

"All the more reason I ain't got no time for his mess," Jimmy said.

Fabrice Dos Veces, who was five-foot-two in her high heels and could barely see over the top of the bar, asked Sabine where Jimmy had got to.

"Sleepin' on the floor here, like a good boy."

"Tough for a man or a woman to get any peace these days," said Fabrice, wetting the tips of her index fingers with her tongue and smoothing down her thick black eyebrows before twisting them up at the ends.

Just as Guitar Slim gave it up to Tony Allen, the door opened and in walked Terry Perez and another member of the Sisters of Clytemnestra named Dogstyle Lou. Ruby's Caribbean was not a regular hangout for the Sisters, so Sabine and Fabrice were surprised to see them.

"You serve real women in here?" Dogstyle Lou asked Fabrice.

"We serve real drinks to real people who can pay for them," Fabrice said. "I don't guess you'd know a real woman if she squatted on this bar and pissed in your glass."

Dogstyle Lou, who was six-one and other than svelte, laughed hard and shook her close-cropped head.

"You know, Terry," she said, "that's what I love about New Orleans, the candor of its citizens. There really ain't another city in this country for tellin' it like it is, as old Aaron Neville never can quit remindin' us."

Dogstyle Lou looked at Sabine Yama and then noticed Jimmy Sermo sprawled on the floor.

"Nice place we done found here, though. Got a bartender don't know if it's Charo or Bela Lugosi, with a cadaver and a part-built dwarf for customers."

Terry Perez went over to Jimmy Sermo and nudged his head with the toe of her right boot.

"He's breathin', I think," she said.

Fabrice billyclubbed Dogstyle Lou so fast the large woman never saw it coming. Sabine grabbed Terry Perez around the throat with his one powerful good hand and squeezed until Terry lost consciousness, then allowed her to drop to the floor next to Jimmy Sermo and Dogstyle Lou. He swiveled back to the bar and finished his drink.

"Care for another, Sabine? On the house."

"No thanks, Fabrice. I'm drivin'."

Sabine twirled off the barstool, stepping carefully over the bodies.

"Be glad to help out here," he said.

"Not necessary, Sabine, but thanks. I can handle it. Do me a favor, though? On your way out."

"What's that?"

"Play 'Lookin' for a Love' again."

"You got it, Fabrice."

Sabine dropped in a quarter, pressed the letter *H* and the number *8,* and hit the street.

THE VISITATION

It was not a rat. Beatifica could tell. A rat might tip over a lamp, there would be a crash, followed by a scurrying sound. This noise was made by a larger creature, she was certain. Beatifica opened her eyes but lay completely still in the dark. There was movement accompanied by a fluttering or shuffling of some kind. At first, it sounded like wings beating, then boxes being pushed along the floor. Beatifica sat up and saw a tall, willowy shape moving slowly on the far side of her room. The shape turned sideways, and in the crooked finger of light from Decatur Street she was able to clearly discern an outline of beard, an aquiline nose. He was wearing a black frock coat, as he always had.

"John!" she said, and the figure froze.

"It's you, John, it must be. Come closer."

The figure turned toward the bed and took one short step, then halted.

"I knew you would come to me, John. I believed that sooner or later you would offer me more than your voice in a dream. I will do what you ask, John. I have the weapon now. There is only the appropriate moment yet to choose."

Beatifica let down the straps of her nightgown, baring her breasts. She spread wide her arms and beckoned with her fingers to the paralyzed form.

"Take me, John," she pleaded. "Long, long have I been only yours. Make love to me now, quickly, while the moonlight lasts."

Beatifica rose and went to him, took hold of his coat and pulled him to the bed, drawing him down upon her.

"John Brown's body lies with me!" she shouted, as her visitor began to move of his own volition.

BEGUILED

The serpent beguiled me, and I did eat,' said Eve. Accordin' to Genesis, anyway. But was it the truth? I say, was woman be*guiled?* Was she in all ways de*ceived?* I think not, people. When Eve partook of the apple, she bit off more'n she could chew, now didn't she? And, folks, I'll tell you—not that you need to be told, but to let you know you're not isolated in your thinkin'—there is no such a thing as an immaculate *de*ception. No such a thing! A woman knows what she's doin' when she does somethin', same as a man. There ain't no difference, none at all. When a woman has sexual intercourse with a man, she knows, has *prior* knowledge, that amongst the results of the commission of the act could be the conception of a child. And once that life exists it has rights just like you or me, foremost of which is the fundamental right to live. If you kill that baby, that's murder. Period.

"Now, I know those who call themselves 'pro-choic-
ers' say, 'What if the pregnancy is the result of a rape?'
Or, 'What if you know the child is defective?' Or, 'What
if the birth poses a threat to the life of the mother?' Or,
'What if the parents are too poor to support it?' Well, I'll
tell you, people—again, not that you need to be told—
killin' is killin'. It's right up there at the top of the list
with 'Thou shalt not steal' and all the rest, isn't it?
'Thou shalt not kill.' You go to them cops 'n' robbers
movies, or watch them silly TV shows, or read comic
books like *The Punisher,* I know. I do it, too. And it's fun
because why? Because you know it's not real! There's
your difference! And it means everything concernin'
what we're talkin' about tonight.

"I am aware that when I speak to you-all about this
that I am preachin' to the already converted, except that
most of you ain't had to be converted. No, most all of you
had the good sense to have it down straight from the
get-go. So this is all I mean to say anymore about it.
What needs discussin' is how to make the blind to see
and cause the lame to walk unaided. Blessed be the one
hand that cleanses the other. How can one hand do the
job right if it don't know what the other hand is doin'?
The meal cannot be properly prepared if one hand be
steady and the other hand be unsteady. People, prayer
alone ain't enough to accomplish this task. You-all got
a mighty load of fearsome studyin' to do!"

Beatifica Brown turned off the radio. Arranged tip to
end in a circle in front of where she knelt on the floor
staring at them were the six sixteen-inch aluminum arrows she had purchased with the air gun from Elvis

Steck. In the center of the circle of arrows was the Stealth weapon itself, zoom scope attached.

In her flat on Pauger Street, Dilys Salt listened to the sign-off of her brother's midnight broadcast. "You have been listening to WGOD," said the announcer, "the voice of God in New Orleans." Dilys missed Terry Perez, who was in the hospital with a severely bruised windpipe. She picked up a book of Terry's that was on the bedside table, *Les Fleurs du Mal* by Charles Baudelaire. Dilys opened it at random and read: *"De Satan ou de Dieu, qu' importe?"*

MS. BROWN TO YOU

Easy Earl eased himself out from behind the wheel of his Mercury Monarch and stood next to the car, stretching his back. The years of loading and unloading bags of mail were taking a toll on his sacrum and ilium. It was time, Earl realized, to find an easier way to make a living. If he could get an industrial injury judgment from a Postal Service–approved doctor, Earl knew, he would have a medical pension coming to him for the rest of his life; plus plenty of time to figure out ways to supplement that income. As soon as his lower back loosened up, Earl Blakey walked into the High Heaven and propped himself up on a stool.

"Crown Royal and milk?" asked the bartender, a new man Earl had not seen before.

"How'd you know?"

"Bufor' tip me. Said you come in reg'lar. Straight-haired brother with a Ray Robinson mustache. I'm Maceo."

"CR an' milk'll do, Maceo. What happen to Buford?"

"Havin' a molar pull."

Maceo set Earl's drink on the bar.

"You seen a small, brown, not-too-ugly woman 'bout my age come in?"

Maceo shook his clean head no.

"Good. I ain't missed her then."

Maceo went off to attend another customer and Earl looked up at the television set above the bar. A perfectly coiffed newscaster, whose light brown hair appeared to have been spray-painted on his head, was talking. The way the man's hair was parted, Earl thought, made it look like a sand trap on a dogleg par four, possibly five.

"A federal appeals court refused today to put the nation's strictest anti-abortion law on the fast track to the United States Supreme Court. The U.S. Court of Appeals in New Orleans denied motions by the state attorney general to expedite a hearing on the issue and to certify issues in the case for immediate Supreme Court review. The three-judge panel gave no reasons for the decision.

"The law passed by the Louisiana State Legislature this summer would send doctors who perform abortions to jail for up to ten years with fines of up to one hundred thousand dollars. It would allow abortions only to save a mother's life or, under strict guidelines, in cases where pregnancy resulted from rape or incest."

Earl sipped on his Crown Royal and milk, then set it down, pulled up a Kool from the pack in his breast pocket and stuck it between his lips. He waited until the newscaster completed the report on the abortion issue before bothering to light his cigarette.

"A U.S. district judge earlier this month ruled that the Louisiana law was unconstitutional. The judge's decision effectively blocked its enforcement until and unless a higher court reverses him. The attorney general stated today: 'Louisiana's position is that the state has not only a rational basis but also a compelling state interest in protecting the life of the unborn.' "

Earl picked up a pack of matches that were on the bar, struck one, touched it to the dangling tip of the Kool and inhaled deeply. He looked at the matchbook and read the words that were printed on the cover: **EARN BIG BUCKS WRITING POETRY! CALL 1-800-RIMBAUD.** Earl had arranged to meet Beatifica at the High Heaven in order to pay her the last of what was owed for Rita's abortion. The woman certainly had done right by Rita, Earl thought, and been nothing but patient concerning remuneration.

"You don't mind I shut this peckerwood down?" Maceo said to Earl, as he reached up and silenced the news. "Heard about enough of women's troubles."

Maceo's question obviously having been of a rhetorical nature, Earl refrained from comment. The bartender went around the bar to the jukebox, dropped in a handful of change and punched a bunch of numbers. The ghostly wail of Stevie Ray Vaughan's steel guitar playing on "Hillbillies from Outer Space" put a decidedly different spin on the atmosphere.

"That ought should make your drink taste better," said Maceo, coming back across from Earl. "Need a refill yet?"

Easy Earl smiled, exposing the seven gold teeth he had paid two grand for to replace his natural ones that a man named DeSoto Sturgis had knocked out of Earl's head with a dog's-head walking stick during an altercation at an after-hours spot called Wig Hat Tippo's up in Itawamba County, Mississippi, twenty years before. Earl had heard shortly thereafter that DeSoto Sturgis was residing for the time being on death row in Angola for shooting out a white woman's eyes in a Bossier City hotel room. Earl did not know for certain if DeSoto Sturgis actually had been electrocuted or not, but he assumed the sentence had been carried out, seeing as how the state of Louisiana had hardly ever hesitated to execute white trash, let alone black men the caliber of DeSoto Sturgis.

"Pour one more," Earl said to Maceo. "I ain't got no new business with this woman I'm waitin' on."

Maceo laughed, displaying his own array of metallic replacement parts. Spying them, Earl figured there had been a DeSoto Sturgis or two in Maceo's past as well.

"You think that," the bartender said, "the woman got you right where she want you."

Easy Earl grinned again and finished off his first CR and milk. Texas steel guitar notes ricocheted inside his cerebral hemispheres.

"Mostly, I say you be right. But this one, uh uh. She walkin' on higher ground."

"Mm, mm, Mr. Earl. Then bet you a Negro dollar we be hearin' her name on the TV news."

Earl nodded and said, "Had me bigger surprises, Maceo, but okay. You on."

THE AWAKENING

When Beatifica was seven years old, an incident occurred the memory of which stayed with her for the remainder of her life. Her father had some business with a man on Okaloosa Street near Nebraska Avenue, and he took his young daughter along with him. It was an extremely hot Sunday afternoon in late August, and as they drove in German Moreno's powder blue Ford Galaxie north through Tampa from Ybor City, the section of town in which they lived, it seemed to Beatifica as if the entire city were on fire. The hazy air was yellow with brown particles floating in it, and the little girl felt like she imagined her goldfish, Bandido, did when the water in his bowl needed to be changed.

At the intersection of Buffalo and Nebraska, a naked man ran out in front of German Moreno's car. German jammed on his brakes, causing Beatifica, who was riding in the front passenger seat and was not wearing a seat belt, to be thrown forward against the dashboard. She cut open her forehead and bruised her nose, but otherwise was unhurt. Beatifica sat back and saw that the naked man, who had long, stringy brown hair and a beard, and was so skinny that the outlines of his bones were visible beneath his skin, was sitting on the hood of her father's Ford. The man was staring directly at her with his unblinking red eyes and sticking out his thick black tongue, which he wagged from side to side.

"Papa! Papa!" Beatifica had cried, diving into her father's arms and burying her bloodied head in his chest.

The naked man next stood up on the car's hood and urinated against the windshield. German Moreno sat transfixed behind the steering wheel, not believing that this could be happening. Beatifica turned and looked at the insane creature perched on the automobile and watched him direct with one hand the spray from his penis to the untinted safety glass. She felt her tears mix with the blood that streamed down her face, but Beatifica did not turn away again. German switched on the windshield wipers and there immediately ensued a series of loud popping noises. The wild man fell sideways, his cock still in his hand, and landed on the street next to the Galaxie's left front tire. Beatifica just stared at the congealing green streaks on the windshield.

By the time she and her father arrived at the house on Okaloosa Street, Beatifica had fallen asleep, her head in German's lap. He shook his daughter gently to awaken her, and the first words Beatifica spoke after opening her eyes were, "Papa, why did Jesus piss on us?"

THE SECRET LIFE OF INSECTS

"You won't believe this, Brother Dallas."

"Believe what? Who's callin' on the damn phone at this ungodly hour, Sabine?"

"It's your sister, Dilys."

Dallas Salt took the portable phone from Sabine Yama and cradled it over the embroidered gold initials scripted on the breast pocket of his purple silk pajamas. He sat straight up in his bed as Sabine propped two pillows behind his back and head. Dallas cleared his throat before raising the receiver to his ear.

"Dilys? To what do I owe this pleasure? Do you know that it's three-thirty in the mornin'?"

"I know the time, Dallas, and there ain't no pleasure involved. I got bad news. Pillara's dead."

"How?"

"Mama said the people at the Thelma Cates Palestine

House in Plain Dealin', where we been keepin' her these years, told her Pillara was on a picnic outin' to the Red River where a tarantula hawk flew into her left ear, got trapped and stung her. By the time they got to a doctor, Pillara was swole up worse'n a 4-H champion bull. Died at four P.M. this afternoon."

"Why'd you wait so long to call me?"

"Wasn't sure I was gonna call at all, seein's how you ain't paid no attention to our daughter since she was born. But I knew Mama would if I didn't, so I told her I would. Now I done it."

"Where's the funeral?"

"Ain't gonna be one. I told the Palestines to let Mama take her for burial in a field between Ida and Mira. That way Mama and her people can tend to the grave."

"What denomination is it?"

"What you suppose? Deep Bottom Baptist, like all Mama's folks."

"We should be there, Dilys. Say some words."

"Maybe be holdin' hands while the pine box is lowered, you think? Fuck you, Dallas."

Dilys hung up. Lightning streaked the sky outside Dallas's bedroom window, but there was no rain.

"Sabine?" said Dallas, passing the crippled Cajun-Pakistani the phone. "You recall that six-foot-tall quadroon female impersonator from Lake Charles moved to New Orleans last year? Name Mumbo Jumbo or somethin'?"

Sabine nodded. "Mumbo Degolas. She from Lake Arthur. Works at Chataignier's Monkey House in the Quarter."

"Call her for me, Sabine, if you please. See she can

come 'round, do a favor. Tell her if I asleep when she get here, just start ahead, wake me up with them fat lips polishin' the knob."

"What about Dilys?"

"She never could give a decent blow job, Sabine. Teeth too big. You just go on, call Miss Mumbo."

Dallas rolled onto his left side and closed his eyes. He remembered a fellow he had been in the service with named Larry Lucca, an Italian boy born in Brooklyn, New York, who claimed he had an uncle from the old country who was afflicted with a disease called tarantism, a nervous condition characterized by melancholy, stupor and an uncontrollable desire to dance. Dallas wondered whether Larry Lucca's uncle had contracted his disease from the sting of a tarantula hawk wasp rather than from the bite of a tarantula spider, which the Lucca family believed had caused the malady.

As Dallas drifted off to sleep, he envisioned a young girl with slanted eyes and a broad, short skull sticking out her large tongue as she clumsily danced the tarantella.

PURPLE NOON

Ever since John Brown's visitation, Beatifica had eagerly awaited his return. Night after night she lay awake until exhaustion overtook her and she fell into a brief and troubled sleep. Beatifica thought it possible that the great man of her life had been waylaid by government agents fearful of the abolitionist's sworn intention to create "a host of Ossawatomies," violent actions directed against areas of recalcitrance concerning equality and progressive behavior. Since being recruited via telepathic communication into this resurgent force of enlightenment, Beatifica had meditated on the meaning of having been infected with the spirit of John Brown, and realized his desires now issued forth through her and others like her. Whether or not he came to her again, Beatifica knew she would rise to meet his expectations.

Every Saturday at noon, Dallas Salt kept an appointment at Dutz's Dancing Comb Barber Shop on Felicity Street. For weeks, Beatifica had surreptitiously observed the preacher's movements, and she decided that it would be in Dutz Sanglant's chair at the Dancing Comb that Brother Dallas's days were to be clipped short.

Following a particularly restless Friday night, Beatifica rose from her companionless sheets slightly after daybreak. It was a chilly, cloudy December 2, the anniversary of John Brown's hanging. The assassin assembled her weaponry, concealing the ordnance in a large canvas Canal Place shopping bag. Beatifica dressed carefully, wearing a tie-dyed, 100-percent cotton T-shirt with the words WHEN DIPLOMACY FAILS printed on the front underneath a tan field-jacket liner. Over this she wore a night desert uniform with a random pattern of scattered dark olive drab splotches and grid lines on a lighter shade of olive drab. Around her waist Beatifica buckled a Type 13 nylon-webbed black aircraft belt, and over her head draped a polyester sniper face veil. She pulled on black Coolmax socks, Sta-Dri liners and a pair of olive drab breathable leather-and-cotton duck jungle boots with non-clogging Panama outsoles and web-reinforcement straps. She stood by the window and studied the sky, seeing no face among the clouds. Beatifica stayed in her room until eleven A.M., at which time she picked up her bag and began the trek toward Felicity Street.

Dallas Salt was in an unusually sour mood this morning. His sleep had been disturbed by a dream wherein

Dilys, dressed in rags, approached him as he stood in front of his congregation on the stage of the Church on the One Hand, and when she opened her mouth as if to speak, a deformed baby emerged head first, falling to the ground at his feet. The baby uttered no sound, but twisted and writhed in apparent agony on the stage as Dallas's flock confronted him, chastising him for having committed an unholy act with his sister. At this point, Dilys was swallowed up by the advancing pack and disappeared. Dallas had awakened in a sweat, his arms stiff at his sides.

"Just a shave today, Dutz," Dallas said, as he assumed his position in the barber's chair. "I don't feel like sittin' for very long."

"Wad chew say, pasta," said Dutz Sanglant, a rail-thin, hairless man of fifty-five whose ocherous skin color betrayed his quarter-century addiction to Pernod. His childhood nickname had been "The Chihuahua."

As Dutz levered the chair backwards, Dallas Salt looked at the faithful Sabine Yama, who sat opposite him beneath the wall-length mirror, reading a back issue of *Soldier of Fortune* magazine, turning the pages with his one normal set of fingers. Dallas's stomach quivered and suddenly he felt nauseated, but he fought the urge to vomit and closed his eyes as the barber wrapped a hot towel around his face.

It was Sabine who first noticed the person, face swathed in see-through cloth, come through the door. Dutz ceased his ministrations as soon as he heard the crinkle of the shopping bag, and looked over just as the initial flash of metal disappeared into the preacher's pancreas. The next missile entered Dutz Sanglant's open mouth and penetrated through the rear of his skull into the wall behind him. A third arrow ripped part of Sabine Yama's face off, sending him to his knees. The fourth and final projectile pierced the leaking and listing pastor's heart, its tip sticking out the back of the chair, stabilizing the body.

As the shrouded figure turned away, the half-blind Yama managed to extricate from his belt a Beretta .25 automatic, which he directed the lethal end of toward the offender and fired as many times as he could before collapsing in pain and losing consciousness, his rent flesh resting on the worn, cool linoleum.

LA VERDAD

None of the Sisters of Clytemnestra had an objection to Dilys's special treatment of Sabine Yama. From the moment Dilys had taken him in, the crippled and severely disfigured man had become an indispensable member of the Church on the Other Hand. He would do anything for Sister Dilys, day or night, and had taken to sleeping on the floor at the foot of her bed. Sabine was Dilys Salt's factotum, her bodyguard, her confidant. She was all he had left in the world in the way of family, Sabine said.

When Terry Perez called him Quasimodo after she had seen Charles Laughton in *The Hunchback of Notre Dame* on the late movie, even Sabine laughed; although it was difficult for anyone to tell that he was laughing, because the mouth improvised for him by the doctors was a small hole where his chin would have been had he still had one. Dilys, however, assured the others that Sabine was not offended by Terry's remark, and, in fact, found the reference not inappropriate.

The demise of the Church on the One Hand had been immediate, vulturous rival preachers having commenced their raiding of Brother Salt's supporters as soon as the news broke that he had fallen. "MADWOMAN MURDERS DALLAS!" shrieked the headline of the *Times-Picayune* on Sunday, December 3. She had slain Dutz Sanglant, too, of course; and Sabine Yama had been accorded the status of a hero for having gunned down the deranged Beatifica Brown. The news of Sabine's miraculous recovery from the six-inch Stealth arrow having gone through one side of his face and out the other had been followed for a while by the local press, but mention of him ceased entirely as soon as it was learned that he had gone to live with Dilys Salt upon his release from the hospital.

Among Sister Dilys's newest devotees was Fatima Verdad, who had been brought into the fold of the Church on the Other Hand by Sabine Yama. On her sixteenth birthday, Fatima had learned that she was HIV positive, and had quit hooking. Knowing that she now had no time to waste in achieving her dream of becoming a popular recording and performing artist, Fatima formed a group called Fatima Verdad and The Band AIDS, comprised solely of musicians afflicted with the disease. The group began by playing at Dilys's services and quickly became a star attraction in New Orleans.

Seized upon by the media as a freakish phenomenon,

the band's notoriety soon spread to New York and Los Angeles, where they were summoned to appear on network and syndicated television shows. Signed to a recording contract by a major company, their first album, "Fatima Verdad and The Band AIDS Take It One Day at a Time," shot to number one on the charts in two weeks. Band members who became too ill to play were replaced only by others infected with HIV. Fatima Verdad spent much of her time visiting AIDS patients in hospitals and hospice situations, and she and the other members of the group donated virtually all of their income to AIDS research and the Church on the Other Hand.

When Fatima finally succumbed to the virus, Sabine Yama was at her bedside. Before she died, Fatima, who was not yet eighteen years old, told him that she could not have expected to derive any more pleasure or satisfaction from life than she already had, but that did not mean she was ready to go. As she held Sabine's withered hand in her right, Fatima felt her lungs suddenly fill with fluid and she started to choke.

"Oh, shit, baby," she gasped, "is this it?"

3

THE BALLAD OF EASY EARL

Everybody's talking, but nobody knows.
—Sonny Boy Williamson

ALFONZO'S MEXICALI

Easy Earl Blakey cruised along Louisiana Avenue in his 1978 Mercury Monarch with all four windows down, his left arm hanging out to catch a breeze and his right hand on the steering wheel. It was Saturday night, just past ten, and Earl had decided to check out the scene at Alfonzo's Mexicali Club. He crossed La Salle Street, pulled over to the curb and parked. It was unseasonably warm for January in New Orleans, the temperature still in the mid-seventies and a humidity reading over eighty. At least two dozen black men of various ages lounged on the street in front of Porky Muette's Port in a Storm Liquor Store, drinking from or holding in one hand a short dog in a brown paper sack. Most of them eyeballed Earl as he got out of his car, which he did not bother to lock, leaving the windows down.

"Evenin', fellas," Easy Earl said, nodding in their direction as he walked toward Alfonzo's Mexicali, which was two doors over.

The men and boys who hung out here lived in the housing project across the street or in one of the several run-down transient hotels on the block. There were a few bad asses among them, but mostly they were just poor folks making time pass more easily with the aid of an inexpensive anesthetic.

"Got a extra dollar, Pop?" a young man of about eighteen asked Earl.

Earl stopped and handed him a five.

"Nothin' extra these days, son," he said. "But I like to find my car how I left it when I come back out."

The young man grinned and took the money.

"Enjoy you self, Cap. Ain nobody gon touch it."

Earl entered the Mexicali and sat down on a stool at the bar. There were a few people dancing, some sitting at the several tables lined along one wall, a couple of others on barstools. It was early yet for Saturday night. By one A.M., Earl knew, the place would be jumping.

"How you, stranger?"

"Just fine, Miz Alfonzo," Earl said to the heavy-set, middle-aged woman bartender who had greeted him in the same manner that she greeted every customer.

"Jim Beam and water?" she asked.

"Crown Royal and milk on the rocks, if you please, ma'am."

"JB's a buck tonight."

"Stick to my standby, CR and milk, thanks."

Miz Alfonzo laughed. "Ain't ever'body afford a extra fo' bits."

She left him his drink, picked up the two dollars he had laid on the bar, and brought back two quarters, which Earl waved away. Miz Alfonzo nodded and smiled, turned and dropped them into a glass next to the cash register, then walked down to the other end of the bar.

Earl sipped at his Crown Royal and milk and listened to the music. A deejay was playing old stuff. Right now was "If You Lose Me, You'll Lose a Good Thing" by Barbara Lynn, a local favorite. Hearing the song made Earl think of his ex, Rita. They had busted up right after her recent abortion. She had gone with her children to live with her sister in Baton Rouge and Earl had not spoken to Rita since.

The door opened and a large Latino man about thirty years old, dressed in an ice cream suit over a maroon shirt and beige tie, a young black woman hanging onto his left arm, entered the Mexicali. They passed Earl and paraded to the other end, stopping opposite Miz Alfonzo. Earl could not hear the initial exchange between them, but then Miz Alfonzo raised her voice, as did the young woman.

"You don't be draggin' yo tacky self in here with no greasy pimp!" shouted Miz Alfonzo. "Take it back out on the street!"

"Luis and me is down, Mama! Get used to it!"

"Get used to this!" Miz Alfonzo said, and pulled up a .38 revolver from behind the bar.

"Take the ho and go!" she yelled at Big Luis, pointing the gun at his chest. "She ain't no mo daughter to me!"

What happened next took place so fast that Earl could not quite follow the action. Several people surrounded

Big Luis, whose white suit became visible only in flashes as the large Latino struggled with them. Somehow, Miz Alfonzo's daughter gained possession of the revolver and tossed it along the top of the bar toward Earl, who made a big mistake: He picked it up.

Earl heard a weird noise coming from behind him, a loud, grinding sound. As he turned around to investigate the source, everything slowed down. White lights popped in Earl's eyes, as if a series of flashbulbs were going off. The floor tilted and Earl lost his balance. His first thought was that someone had kicked the stool out from under him, but he did not fall down. Then came the moaning—long, slow, unearthly noises unlike anything he had ever heard before. The air was full of multi-colored feathers that covered everything.

Easy Earl had no idea how he came to be in his car, driving on Palmetto Street toward Metairie. His left cheek burned and he touched it, then glanced at the blood on his fingers. The .38 was on the seat next to him.

Back at Alfonzo's Mexicali Club, the policeman who had been wounded in the abdomen asked the woman kneeling by his head if his partner was all right. She told him that the other officer looked pretty dead and to lie still, an ambulance was coming.

"Who shot us?" asked the wounded man. "And why?"

The woman shook her head and said, "Honey, I just don't know."

HELLO, WILLIE!

"Earl, my man, it's a god-damn good thing you got a big dick," Easy Earl Blakey said aloud, as he sat alone in his car on the side of the road by Irish Bayou, " 'cause you sure must have a tiny motherfuckin' brain."

He had no idea what time it was, but Earl figured it had to be well past midnight by now. He had been driving aimlessly around the city since fleeing Alfonzo's Mexicali, and finally pulled over due to fatigue. What had gone down back there? he asked himself. All he could remember was that there had been some kind of an argument at the other end of the bar, and then the gun spinning along the mahogany into his hand. He had heard someone coming up behind him, turned and saw two guns pointed in his direction. After that, Earl's mind was blank. He knew he had fired the revolver, though, even if he could not clearly recall having done so. Something in his brain had just snapped when he'd seen those pistols pushed toward his face.

He took a deep breath, then lit up a Kool. There was so little traffic out here, he thought, looking up at the crescent moon. If he shot himself, it might be two or three days, maybe a week, before his body would be discovered. Earl sat and smoked. When he had had enough of it, he tossed the butt out the window, then picked up the revolver and got out of the car. Earl walked over to the bayou and threw the gun into the water. He stood there for a minute, listening. All he heard were airplane engines droning overhead. Earl went back to the Mercury, got in and cranked it up. Where to? he wondered, and started driving.

For some reason, the image of Willie Wong entered Earl's mind. Willie Wong had been a boyhood pal of Earl's. They had grown up together in the Eighth Ward and remained friends until Willie's death at the age of twenty-one. Willie had been a normal Chinese-American kid; he had studied hard in school and worked regularly at various jobs to help support himself and his parents, who owned a small grocery store on St. Claude Avenue. Then, when Willie was eighteen, he saw the movie *The Wild One,* which starred Marlon Brando as a devil-may-care, hardcase motorcycle gang leader. Willie fell in love with the image personified by Brando, and he bought a thirdhand Triumph Bonneville, allowed his lank black hair to grow long, wore a leather jacket, engineer boots and oily Levi's. He also started smoking, something else he never had done before, and it was rare to see him riding around on his bike without an unfiltered Lucky Strike dangling from his lips. Willie even invented his own nickname, "the Wild Wong," and encouraged everyone he knew to call him that. Only his parents refused to honor this request, continuing to address him as they always had, by his Chinese name, Zhao.

The Wild Wong was killed on a wet Thursday evening when a drunken driver in a brand-new SAAB sedan cut too closely in front of Willie's Triumph on Chef Menteur Highway and clipped the front wheel, catapulting the Wild Wong headfirst into a roadside ditch, breaking his back and neck. At Willie's funeral, Earl had been surprised to see that the Wong family had dressed their son in his biker clothes to be viewed in an open casket. He had been certain that the Wongs would have cut Willie's hair and put him into a suit. As he passed the casket, Earl had noticed that an unsealed package of Lucky Strike cigarettes had been placed in Willie's left hand.

Why he thought at this difficult moment in his own life of the Wild Wong, Earl did not know. Something had happened to Willie when he'd seen that movie, and his life had been changed irrevocably. Now, Easy Earl knew, nothing would be the same for him, either. That was it, he supposed. Something a person never could imagine took place and then the world looked completely different.

The image of Willie Wong lying in his coffin twenty-five years ago would not go away, and Earl drove fast on the deserted road in his Monarch with the headlights off.

"Whoooeeee! Willie Wild Wong, you dumb motherfucker!" Earl shouted. "I'm comin' to find you, brother, ready or not!"

NIGHT OWL

It was slightly after four A.M. when Earl Blakey drove into a Red Devil service station outside Tornado, Mississippi. He had driven north-northeast from Irish Bayou on the old two-lane highway, U.S. 11, across Lake Pontchartrain and the Pearl River, past Picayune and Carriere to Poplarville, where he had swung west on Mississippi State Road 43 and decided to stop for fuel before crossing back into Louisiana.

There was a light burning in the station office, and Earl hoped somebody was around so that he could keep going. He cut the engine, turned off the lights and got out of the car. A swarm of stinging insects descended on him in the darkness and Earl swatted at them as he walked toward the office. Through the glass in the door, Earl saw a white man seated on the floor, his back against a wall. There was a noose around the man's neck, a thick rope strung from a large hook that had been screwed into the ceiling. The man, whose Coke bottle–thick eyeglasses were askew and who was wearing an oil-stained white-and-black Ole Miss baseball cap, was either asleep or dead. Earl could not tell, although there seemed to be no discernible movement, no rise and fall of the man's chest.

Earl tried to open the door but it was locked. To enter, he would have had to break the glass, and he did not need any more trouble tonight. He looked again at the man, who appeared to be in his forties, wondering how he could be dead if he was sitting on the floor instead of hanging in the air. The rope was knotted at the top around the hook and had plenty of slack in the line down to the noose. Then Earl noticed the black letters on the floor at the ends of the man's outstretched legs, and that both of the man's feet were missing. He pressed closer to the glass and read the words that had been spraypainted there: EL MOCHUELO.

"Damn," Earl said. "Guess I got enough gas to get to Bogalusa."

He hurried back to his car, got in and drove away.

ROADRUNNER

"Interestin' license plate you got there," the attendant in the 76 station in Bogalusa said. "EZY EARL. That you?"

Earl Blakey handed the kid a ten and a five.

"Used to was, an' maybe not even," said Earl.

The kid laughed. "I hear dat!"

Earl knew where he was headed now and he took 21 South out of town. At Covington, he'd take 190 West, stay off the interstate. As he sped past Sun, Louisiana, over the Bogue Chitto River, Earl considered the possibility that the last twelve hours of his life had been a dream; that he had not really shot two policemen in Alfonzo's Mexicali Club in New Orleans, and not seen a footless white man with his head in a noose on the floor of a Red Devil gas station outside Tornado, Mississippi. Maybe he was suffering from a medical condition and he could get a doctor to explain it. Rita and her sister, Zenoria Rapides, would help him, he figured, which was why he was on his way to Baton Rouge.

Earl still did not entirely understand why Rita had acted strangely toward him after her abortion. They had discussed the situation beforehand, agreed that it was the best solution, her being thirty-six years old and already having four children. Earl had paid for it, treated her kindly, but then Rita got bitter and took off quick up to Zenoria's. He was puzzled about that, but now it was himself, Mr. Earl, who needed backup, and he hoped Rita would be there for him.

Earl turned on the radio.

"The long-lost gun tied to the assassination of former governor of Louisiana Huey P. Long fifty-six years ago has been found. James Starrs, a forensic scientist who plans to exhume the body of the purported assassin, Carl Austin Weiss, Sr., said in Washington, D.C., where he is a professor at George Washington University, that the .32-caliber handgun allegedly used to kill 'the Kingfish' in the Louisiana State Capitol in 1935 is in the possession of Mabel Guerre Binnings, the seventy-five-year-old daughter of the policeman who investigated the case. Binnings lives in New Orleans.

"Professor Starrs says he is certain the discovery of the apparent murder weapon will prove to be 'a bonanza of evidence.' The disclosure, however, has set off a legal battle over who owns the gun and the police files on the case, which also have been missing since 1940 when Mabel Binnings's father, Louis Guerre, retired.

"Louisiana State Police insist that both the weapon

and the files belong to the people of Louisiana, and have delivered a letter requesting that Mabel Binnings hand them over. She has refused this request and has also declined to talk to reporters. Ever since the shooting in Baton Rouge, there has been speculation that Long, who was forty-two years old at the time, actually died from bullets fired by his bodyguards. The twenty-nine-year-old Weiss was gunned down by them on the Capitol steps."

Easy Earl lit a Kool, found a pair of dark glasses in the glove box and put them on. They were Rita's. Earl recalled the time he had bought them for her in the Walgreen's on Royal.

"In New Orleans," the radio news continued, "the manhunt for the killer of a metro police officer is underway. A second officer was wounded in the incident, which took place last night at Alfonzo's Mexicali Club on Louisiana Avenue. Details regarding the circumstances of the shootings are still unclear, said Acting Police Commissioner DuMont 'Du Du' Dupre. The suspect is believed to be a middle-aged black male with a pencil-thin mustache who may be driving a red late-1970s Mercury automobile. No further information is presently available.

"We have an appropriate tune comin' right up, people. 'I Am a Lonesome Fugitive,' sung by Ferriday, Louisiana's own bad boy, Jerry Lee Lewis. But first we have to pay a few bills."

Earl turned off the radio. He drove straight through to Baptist, where he stopped in a 7-Eleven and bought a Bic razor, a Snickers bar and a black corduroy Playboy bunny baseball cap. He dry-shaved in the car, using the rearview mirror, then ate the candy bar. This was the first time since he was sixteen years old, Earl realized, that he had not worn a mustache. He put on the bunny hat, adjusted his dark glasses, and hoped he could make it to Zenoria's house on Mohican Street in Baton Rouge before the cops caught him.

WOMEN ARE WOMEN BUT MEN ARE SOMETHING ELSE

Zenoria Rapides had never married. Now forty-seven years old, she had lived alone, until Rita and the children arrived, in a two-bedroom house that she had bought and mostly paid for with her earnings as a grade-school teacher and seamstress. Her reputation as a dressmaker was nonpareil among the middle-class white women of Baton Rouge, and they brought her more work than she could adequately handle. Zenoria was pleased that her youngest sister, Rita Hayworth Rapides, had come to live with her, since Rita sewed almost as well as Zenoria herself and was willing to assist in the business.

There had been six children born to Althea Yancey and Zelmo Baptiste Rapides: Zenoria, Zelma and Zoroaster were named by their father; and Althea had named Lana Turner, Pocahantas and Rita Hayworth.

Althea and Zelmo had perished sixteen years ago when their house on Evangeline Street, in which all of the children had been raised, caught fire due to an electrical problem and burned down in the middle of one night with them trapped inside. Zelma and Zoroaster, who were identical twins, were killed together in a car crash coming back from Port Allen, where they worked in a Popeye's, when they were sixteen. Lana Turner now lived in Memphis, married to a radical white lawyer named Lucius Lamar Bilbo, a great-nephew of the former Mississippi senator who had advocated deportation of all southern blacks to Africa. Zenoria and Rita seldom heard from her. Pocahantas had disappeared at the age of seventeen with a dishwasher from the Poteat Cafe in downtown Baton Rouge named Leopard Johnny, so called due to his peculiar black-and-yellow complexion, the result of a chronic, debilitating liver condition. The only word of Pocahantas that Zenoria or Rita or Lana had received in the last fifteen years was a picture card of the Monongahela River sent to Zenoria, postmarked Pittsburgh, Pennsylvania, that said, "Dere Sister, The Leopard has Lost his Spots. Hi to All. Love, Pokey."

Rita Hayworth Rapides's four children were the progeny of four different fathers, none of whom had Rita married, though at least two had proposed to her. Rita enjoyed her independence and insisted that each child carry her own surname. She had named them after four western states—Montana, Wyoming, Idaho and Colorado—none of which had she visited, nor was she particularly interested in visiting them. She told Zenoria that she just liked the sounds of the names.

Rita found that she usually had no use for men beyond occasional companionship. She preferred, also, to support herself; not that she ever refused financial help from any of the children's fathers, but Rita never depended on it. Until Easy Earl Blakey came around, she had not really been tempted to maintain a close friendship with a man. There was something uncomplicated about Blakey, Rita thought; not simple, exactly, but he was—true to his nickname—easy to be with. The termination of this recent pregnancy, her first abortion, had depressed Rita more than she ever could have anticipated. She had moved back to Baton Rouge just to have the comfort of her oldest sister, not to escape from Earl or New Orleans. Rita missed Earl, which surprised her; and when he turned up on Zenoria's doorstep that Sunday morning, clean-shaven and wearing a stupid Playboy bunny hat, Rita took him into her arms without a word and felt her entire body relax.

"They after me, Rita," Earl said, once they were inside the house. "Where Zenoria and the kids?"

"At church. I wasn't feelin' up to goin'. I ain felt up to goin' most places, lately. Oh, Earl, I am pleased to see you. Why'd you shave your mustache? And what you mean, they after you? 'They' who?"

"Po-lice. I shot a cop, Rita. Two cops. One's dead, other's wounded."

"Earl, you talkin' crazy. Easy Earl Blakey don't go around smokin' nobody, 'specially policemens."

"I know, honey, but it happen. I was havin' a CR an' milk in Alfonzo's Mexicali, by myself, thinkin' on you an' how much I been missin' us, when the incident just

come about. That's all, it just come about. Next thing I
find, I'm runnin'. I went to Miss'ippi firs', seen somethin'
there so awful I ain sure I really seen it."

"Wait, baby. You talkin' too fast. How you so sure you
shot anyone?"

"Had the gun with me in my car after it happen."

"You don't own no piece, Earl. Where's this gun?"

"Throwed it in Irish Bayou. It belong to Miz Alfonzo."

"Bad idea. Be some Cambo fish it out the bayou fo'
long."

"That don't matter, Rita. Prob'ly a bad idea me comin'
here, too, but I been missin' you so much. They bound to
figure out where I am. They knowin' the car, said on the
radio. Shit, Rita, this whole thing just some crazy accident, an' now my life be over."

"Earl, hush. We work it out."

"Rita, I love you." Earl kissed her softly on the lips.
"But ain no way to deal with it 'cept run. You holdin'
any green?"

"About ninety dollars. You can have it."

Rita went into another room and came back out with
the money and handed it to Earl. He kissed her again,
deeply this time.

"I been thinkin' about our baby," he said.

"Thinkin' what?"

"That we shoulda had it. Now I'm gone be dead an' ain
no child of mine in the world to remember me. Also that
if you ain move to Baton Rouge, which you wouldn't of
if we ain kill the baby, I never would of been in the
Mexicali Club in the firs' place."

"Earl, hold it. If you think runnin's the only way, go

on ahead. I don't be stoppin' you or nobody, 'cludin' my children, they own time come, from doin' what they think they got to. But subtractin' out that way won't kick it. Look straight, Earl. You a good man, I know. I mighta had that baby, you'd told me to."

"You could come with me, Rita. Kids be safe with Zenoria an' we get 'em later."

"Go 'head, Earl. Don't need that nobody be lyin' to the police about not seein' you but me."

Rita kissed him and touched the tip of her right index finger above his upper lip.

"You get where you're goin'," she said, "grow that mustache back."

Earl grinned. "I will, baby."

Rita watched him drive away, then went into the bedroom she shared with Idaho and Colorado—Montana, her oldest, slept in the front room, and Wyoming with Zenoria—and lay down. Suddenly, she felt very tired. Rita remembered her mother, Althea, telling her when she could not have been more than eight years old, that just when things seemed almost to be makin' sense, a damn cow would jump over the moon. Rita had asked, "Whose cow, Mama?" Rita laughed now, lying on the bed, as Althea had twenty-eight years before in response to Rita's question, the only answer her mother had to give.

MARBLE

Earl had heard or read that when the Mafia kidnaps someone and murders him, they usually leave his car at an airport parking lot, so that's what Easy Earl did with his Mercury Monarch, abandoning it at Baton Rouge Metro and riding a bus downtown to the Greyhound terminal. He bought a ticket to Tampa, Florida, a city he'd never been to but one that he figured was big enough for him to find work in. His bus would not leave for forty-five minutes, so he bought a sausage and a Delaware Punch at a concession stand and took a seat in the waiting room.

A thin white girl, about thirteen or fourteen years old, wearing bluejeans and a powder blue LSU sweatshirt, carrying a small canvas bag, came in and sat down on the bench directly across from Earl. The girl's hair was white-blonde, she wore glasses, and she surveyed the waiting room calmly, her unmarked face expressionless. Earl noticed her but his thoughts were connected with his own situation. He ate his sausage and drank the punch and then went to the restroom. By the time he had used the toilet and washed his hands and face, the bus was loading and Earl climbed aboard. He took an aisle seat, three-quarters of the way toward the rear, next to the young white girl.

The bus was five minutes out of Baton Rouge on Interstate 12 when the girl said to Earl, "My name is Marble Lesson, I'm from Bayou Goula, though my daddy lives up in New Roads now, and I'm on my way to meet my mama and her new husband in Jacksonville, Florida. I was born in Miami County, Kansas, where my daddy's people had a farm outside Osawatomie, but they lost it, so we moved to Louisiana where Daddy's cousin Webb got Daddy a job in a refinery. Mama moved out of our house in Bayou Goula months ago, but I wanted to finish the semester since it had already started, so I stayed with Daddy for the time bein'. He didn't could use that big of a house, so he found him a place up at New Roads, in Labarre, actually, in Pointe Coupee Parish, as I said, and dropped me off just now at the bus station.

"My ambition is to be a writer of fiction. I never have got other than a A in English since the fourth grade. I am what is commonly called a keen observer, which means, of course, that I notice details most everyone else don't. Eyeglasses don't bother me. I got 'em five years ago, when I was nine, to perk up my left eye, which is lazy. But my own good guess is that it's the one sees the really important things and the right eye is mostly used to get me from here to there. The eye is a photoreceptor, which means a camera if you can capture what you see and store the image in the cortex, which is the outer layer of the anterior cerebral hemispheres of the brain. My cortex is overflowin' with captives, such as black vomit, one of the most serious symptoms of yellow fever, which I seen a film of victims of in the eighth grade and never forgot, nor will I. It's bound to come in useful for a novel or story before I'm through. Where are you goin'?"

"Tampa," said Earl.

"You'll have to transfer to another bus, then, because this one goes straight through to Jacksonville. Did they tell you that at the terminal? Sometimes people don't volunteer information very readily."

Earl nodded. "Uh huh. Change in Lake City."

"Did I tell you my name? Marble Lesson? Of course, I did. My daddy's name is Wesson, so people call him Wes. My mama's first name is Bird. Her first last name was Arden, like the forest. Then, as you know, it was Lesson. Now it's Doig, which she says nobody can pronounce properly when they see it, so she gets called Bird Dog a lot in Jacksonville. What's yours?"

"Earl."

"Oh my friends they call me Speedo but my real name is Mister Earl."

"Say what?"

"Song Mama used to sing me when I was little."

"Oh yeah, yeah. I kinda do remember it."

Earl closed his eyes.

"You appear to be tired, Mr. Earl."

"Guess I am, Miz Lesson."

"Call me Marble, please."

"Miz Marble. You don't mind awfully, I'mo sneak on out here fo' bit, get some res'."

"I'll wake you up if you're asleep when we get to Lake City, though I doubt you will be since it's hours away."

Earl pulled the black corduroy bunny cap down over his eyes and drifted into a dreamscape where Rita, wearing black lace underwear, was standing over a fiery pit poking at something with a long stick. Earl tried to see what was in the pit, but he could not raise himself high enough. Rita kept jabbing with the stick, and then she speared an object and lifted it out of the pit, gripping the stick with both hands. She held up a charred baby, its limbs outstretched but motionless. Pieces of the corpse flaked off and were carried away by the wind until there was nothing left. Rita dropped the stick into the fire.

SOMETHING SPECIAL

BUS CRASHES, BURNS IN LIGHTNING STORM

GULFPORT, Jan. 21 (SNS)—A Greyhound bus, en route from Baton Rouge, La., to Jacksonville, Fla., was struck by lightning yesterday during a thunderstorm at approximately four P.M. as it traveled on Interstate 10 north of Bay St. Louis, Miss. The strike caused the bus to crash into a roadside ditch, killing twelve passengers and the driver, who was identified as Dio Bolivar, 42, of Phenix City, Ala.

Witnesses said it appeared that the secondary channel of a double bolt of ground lightning struck the bus, which was several miles away from the primary channel that destroyed a railroad bridge-tender's shack just west of Waveland, Miss.

Ten of the eleven survivors were injured, some seriously, and were taken to nearby hospitals for treatment. The only passenger who emerged unhurt was Marble Lesson, 14, of Bayou Goula, La.

Interviewed at the scene, Miss Lesson, who was traveling alone, told rescuers, "A violet vein of hellfire reached down inside the bus and cooked them folks. There was a nice black man sitting next to me and all of a sudden he lit up like a Christmas tree. It was pretty spectacular.

"I don't know why I was spared, except perhaps the Lord has something special planned for me to accomplish in life."

JESUS SEES US

Dear Jesus,

There is no doubt in my brain that it was a direct act of God that I am alive and in fact did escape unscathed and unscarred from the bus crash that took so many lives of the innocent and injured so many others. That I am safe now in the home of my mama Bird Arden and her second husband Fernando Doig on Trout River Boulevard in Jacksonville Florida a town about which I know practically nothing at all since I am a recent arrival is without question a miracle. The Earth cannot turn fast or slow enough to disturb me as I am at this moment as of now undisturbable.

In case You may not know very much about me though I believe You observe us all let me explain just who it is is writing You this letter. I am Marble Lesson (no middle name) 14 years old. Until now I lived in

Bayou Goula Louisiana the state where my daddy Wes still lives. Now I have come to live with my mama and it was while traveling here on the Greyhound that the accident occurred that convinced me of Your investment in me. Writing is how I have chosen to justify Your faith and commitment. You may ask what can a 14 year old girl of The South have to say that You should pay any attention to? I believe writing is a process of self discovery and each thought is my own. Stick with me Jesus You may hear something You never thought of Yourself.

I am concerned about the World Condition not only as things are in my own country of the United States of America but all over the globe. One thing I would like to know is if You see what is going on on other planets or just Earth? A few days ago before I left Bayou Goula on that fateful trip I wrote a song I wish You could hear me sing but maybe You can when I do anyway here are the words.

> *Jesus sees us even when we're bad*
> *And every time I think of that*
> *It makes me feel so glad*
> *Gives me the finest feeling*
> *That I ever have had*
> *Oh Jesus sees us even when we're bad*

In time I plan to add more verses but I thought as long as I have it this far and I am writing to You anyhow You would be interested.

There is a black man staying with our family now at the house who is a friend of Fernando Doig. The black

man's name is Mr. Rollo Lamar and he and Fernando
are lawyers. They are working together for a women's
group in the state of Florida that is pro choice which
means they are for allowing women to decide for themselves as individuals whether or not to have a baby. I am
only 14 but I do not understand how anyone can tell
anyone else what to do with their own body. Personally
I do not know what I would do if I was pregnant and did
not want the baby either have an abortion or have the
baby and give it out for adoption like Lástima Denuedo
did back in Bayou Goula at the age of 15 however I
would want to be able to choose for myself which is only
fair. Others of course do not agree.

Last night at dinner Mr. Lamar told Fernando and
Mama and me about a trial up in Georgia where a man
wore his Ku Klux Klan costume which includes a white
robe like one You wore when You were here on Earth
and a pointy hood and a mask. This man wore this outfit
of the Klan which is a group who hate Jewish people (I
know You are one) and black and other peoples of color
and Catholic persuasion and are against abortion in any
form I am sure to test a law that says it is illegal to wear
a mask in public. Of course at Mardi Gras in New Orleans where I have been many times people always wear
masks so it is no surprise to me that the Ku Klux Klan
person won the case. The argument against him was
that wearing the costume and mask was intended to
strike fear and terror into the minds of the Jewish and
Catholic and black people of the town where he did it.
My thinking about masks is that if every person wore
the same kind of mask and all looked alike then people

would have to deal with who the other person really is on their insides and maybe it would not be such a horrible idea to try someday. That way you would not know if another person is even black or white underneath the mask it is just a person. What do You think?

It is very late at night now and I am pretty sleepy so I will stop here. My plan is to continue writing letters to You until I know where to send them or can deliver them in person. All for now.

Sincerely, your friend

Marble Lesson

4

THE CRIME OF MARBLE LESSON

I am breached by fate,
Wrecked, swept away by storm. You'll pay the price,
Poor people, with your sacrilegious blood.
This wickedness will haunt you, and the grim
Punishment . . . will come home to you,
But it will be too late to pray the gods.

—Virgil, *The Aeneid*

THE GOOD SAMARITAN

Wesson Lesson staggered out of the Saturn Bar into the street. After losing his job in New Roads, Wes had come to New Orleans to visit his brother, Webb, only to learn that Webb had been arrested and jailed for operating a tax scam involving false bills of sale for automobiles. This swindle landed Webb a ten spot at the Atchafalaya Correctional Facility, to which he was sent a week after Wes got to town.

Wes moved into his brother's house on Rocheblave Street and immediately thereafter fell off the wagon on which he had been a brief passenger. His heavy drinking and abusive behavior had cost him his wife, Bird, and their daughter, Marble, and any number of oil field jobs. He was thirty-nine years old, looked fifty, and was definitely headed down the road feeling bad.

Wobbling on the corner of St. Claude Avenue and Clouet Street at two o'clock in the morning, Wes Lesson was suddenly overcome by feelings of guilt about having failed his family, and he dropped to his knees and wept. Marble, who was now fourteen, had gone to live with Bird and her new husband, an attorney named Fernando Doig, in Jacksonville, Florida, and Wes despaired of ever seeing his only child again. He knew he was no good, had mistreated the one woman he had truly loved, forcing her to leave him, and now his beloved daughter was also beyond his touch. Wes lay crumpled up on the broken sidewalk, sobbing, oblivious to the perilous position he was in.

"Best be gettin' on your feet, fella," a large, moon-faced man said, as he reached down to assist Wes Lesson. "You must ain't be up on the local geography. Natives have you skinned in fifteen minutes, spear through your ear, I leave you be."

The man, who appeared to be in his mid-fifties but was still built like a middle linebacker in his prime, lifted Wes with one arm and looked at his puffy face and blood-shot eyes.

"Bud, you in a ugly condition. I'll take you to home, you got one."

"Rochebla' Stree'," Wes said, struggling to stand on his own.

The big man guided Wes to a midnight blue Buick Roadmaster and stuffed him into the front passenger seat, closed the door, then went around to the driver's side and slid behind the wheel.

"Don't know how a man can let this happen to him,"

the driver said, as he pulled the Buick into the sparse traffic on St. Claude. "You smell bad, boy. It's the stink of defeat."

All Wes Lesson could do was groan. He barely heard what his savior of the moment was saying.

"My name's Defillo Humble. Maybe you've heard of me. Wrote a book some years ago did a little. Twenty weeks on the *Picayune* best-seller list. *Negroes with Cars.* About how the African American's access to the automobile drove the final nail into the coffin of the Old South. I'm workin' on a new one now, *The Unnecessary Passing of the Southern Woman.* You can pretty much guess what-all it's about."

Wes Lesson was incapable of intelligent or intelligible response. He was only vaguely aware of what was happening, and when the car stopped in front of his brother's house, Wes could do no better than open the passenger door and drop onto the street. Defillo Humble got out and came around, picked him up and half-carried him to the porch, where he deposited Wes on the top step.

"Best I intend to do, pardner," said Defillo Humble. "Whatever it is you're afraid of, there's worse. Mister, unless you've been forced to eat rodent sushi from the scooped-out skull of a Liberian rebel soldier, like I have, or had a twenty-foot-long anaconda jump into your dugout and swallow half of your five-year-old son before you could put a nine-millimeter round through the serpent's ganglion, like happened to me, you ain't got a clean bone to pick, I don't reckon. I'll get back by sometime, check on you."

Defillo Humble walked to his Roadmaster, got in and drove away. Before the big man got to the next corner, Wes Lesson had fallen asleep right where Defillo had dropped him.

THE MISSION

Dear Jesus,

Daddy called tonight from N.O. where he has gone to live after things didn't work out up at New Roads like he thought but Mama would not allow me to speak with him so I ran upstairs and quietly picked up the extension and listened to their conversation. Jesus it was so awful! Daddy was crying and begging Mama to send me back there to him he doesn't have anyone and he might as well be dead he said. Also Uncle Webb is gone to jail for ten years and Mama said it was about time maybe someone inside the walls will kill him and save the state the trouble.

My tears were running down my face and into the little holes in the mouth part of the telephone and I couldn't stop them. I am sure even You would have been upset at hearing Daddy cry like that. Mama screamed that he was never no good and if I went back there he would probably beat me up some night when he got drunk so Mama swore he would never ever see me again if she could help it. Daddy would not beat on me Jesus I know this.

Jesus when I was with Daddy he did not take a drink the whole time and we done fine together. Now I could tell he had been drinking again and I know if I was with him he would not be so You guessed it I am going to N.O. He is staying in Uncle Webb's house which I know the address so that will not be a problem finding it. The problem is to get there. Since I don't have enough money for a bus I have decided to hitch hike a dangerous decision I suppose but the choice is mine I believe not Mama's. I do not have any friends to speak of in Jacksonville anyway yet so there is nobody here to miss me. Tomorrow instead of going to school I will take a detour.

Please Jesus protect me on the highway on my mission to Daddy. He is not a bad man and needs me more than Mama does so I got to go he don't have another soul to help him. Jesus keep me safe so I won't be sorry.

Your friend,

Marble

SISTERS

Thank you, ma'am. Didn't think anybody was gonna stop for me."

Marble pushed away her white-blonde bangs and smiled at the woman driver who had just picked her up. The woman was black, kind of old—in her sixties, Marble guessed—and she was wearing a hot pink pants suit, rhinestone-decorated dark glasses and a sombrero-type hat with yellow and green feathers sticking out of it. She was driving a brand-new black Cadillac Eldorado with cream leather interior.

"How long have you been waiting, child?" the driver asked. She had an unusually deep voice for a woman, Marble thought.

"Hour or more, I guess."

Marble wore red jeans, a red sweatshirt, red high-top sneakers and her tanker jacket with the orange side out.

She had dressed this way not only for comfort but so that she would be more readily spotted by drivers. Marble carried only her blue school backpack, which was stuffed with extra clothes, toiletries, writing pads and pens.

"It is definitely out of the ordinary to see a young lady such as yourself hitchhiking on the entry ramp to the interstate. I'm surprised a state trooper didn't pick you up."

"Didn't see one. How far are you goin'?"

"My destination is Chattahoochee, where I'm going to visit my son, who is a resident of the institution there. What about yourself?"

"I'm goin' to see my daddy in New Orleans."

"My land, all the way to New Orleans, Louisiana! That's quite a long distance to hitchhike. I don't mean to pry, but do your parents know that you're doing this?"

"No, ma'am, they don't. But my daddy's in a mess and I gotta go to him. He ain't got but me, really. Mama's with a new man now, and she and Daddy don't get along very well."

"I know how these things are," the driver said, nodding her head. "My name is Mrs. Arapaho White. What's yours?"

"Marble Lesson."

"And how old are you, Marble?"

"Fourteen."

"Well, Marble, I am fifty years older than you are, but I can clearly recall what I was like at your age. In fact, fourteen was one of the most important years of my life."

"What happened?"

"Oh, my land! That was when I first really knew that I was a girl trapped in a boy's body."

"Huh? Trapped how?"

"On the exterior I was male, but on the interior I was female. After I figured out that God had made the mistake, things became much easier for me."

"You mean like other kids made fun of you before then?"

"Honey, that was the least of it. No, I mean that I was very confused. I was attracted to boys just like any other girl, only I looked like a boy."

"I can certainly see how that could have caused some problems."

"Did it! Leave me alone with that!"

"So what did you do? I mean, when you were fourteen."

"Just decided to live my life as a woman. Didn't want no operations, either, so's I would altogether resemble a woman. I was pleased with my body and didn't want some doctor cuttin' on it. There was no reason, I figured, not to simply carry on as I was.

"I remember being in church," Arapaho White continued, "when the thought occurred to me that Jesus and Mary Magdalene and John the Baptist, they all of 'em were mistakes, just like me. Freaks, in fact. And they had to do what they had to do, once they realized what that was. From that day forward I have lived as a woman."

"What did your folks think?"

"When I told my mother what I had decided, she plain

passed out. Fainted dead away. My father was long gone. I was told that he'd left shortly after I was born and went to Chicago. My mother and I lived with her parents in Egypt City, Florida. My mother is still there to this day. She's eighty-four years old."

"What did you do?"

"Ran off, of course. I went to Miami and got a job cleaning hotel rooms. I did some other things, too, in order to survive. Not such wonderful things. But I knew who I was and I had faith that everything would turn out right in the end. It has, too, except for Frenesi. He's my son I'm on my way to see at Chattahoochee. His head never has been right, not since he was born."

"Pardon me for askin', but are you his mother or father?"

Arapaho laughed. "Good question, child. Frenesi's natural mother was a Cuban named Esquerita Alvarez. She was a singer, had a gorgeous voice, but her mentality was not all that sound. I guess it was a long-standing affliction in her family. The dementia, I mean. Esquerita and I lived together for about two years. This was in Belle Glade. Then, after Frenesi was born, and Esquerita saw that he wasn't right, she split and left him with me. Esquerita's and my relationship had a few unresolved areas, also, which disturbed her. Anyway, I took care of Frenesi until he was old enough to get into serious trouble.

"I was married by then, to a wonderful man who understood my situation and realized that love involves the person, not the body and its accoutrements. My husband did all he could for Frenesi, but it truly was a lost cause. Frenesi went on a killing spree one night with an Uzi, murdered sixteen people in a Winn-Dixie in Tampa. He told the police that he was defending the Earth against aliens from other planets who were using the Winn-Dixie supermarket as their headquarters."

"That must have been a pretty big disappointment for you, when your son shot all those people. But it's not like parents are altogether responsible for what their children do. I mean, if I robbed a bank or something, I'm the one done it, not Bird or Wes. I'm the one responsible, not them."

"You're a bright girl, Marble. You'll go far."

"It's too bad for me you're not goin' all the way to New Orleans, Mrs. White. I like talking and riding with you."

"Why thank you, Marble. I'm sorry I'm not, too. But I will make it easier for you to get there. I'll take you to the airport in Tallahassee and buy you a ticket to New Orleans. That way you'll be with your father much sooner."

"Oh, Mrs. White, I don't know how or when I could pay you back!"

"Don't worry about it, dear. I have plenty of money. Besides, sisters have to help each other out whenever we can. Remember that."

BIRD CALLS

ho's there?"

"Finally! Wesson, is Marble there?"

"Oh, it's you, Bird. Yeah, she's here. We're about to fix supper."

"My lord, Wesson! We've been frantic, thinkin' Marble been kidnapped or murdered on her way to school yesterday mornin'!"

"Showed up at the door last night. Couldn'ta been more surprised myself, Bird. Thought maybe you'd changed your mind about things."

"Wesson, put Marble on the line.

"Can you believe it?" Bird said to Fernando Doig, while she waited for her daughter to come to the phone. "Marble's been there since last night!"

"Hello, Mama. I'm all right."

"Marble, how did you get to New Orleans so fast?"

"A nice person picked me up when I was hitchhikin' and drove me to the airport in Tallahassee. She bought me a plane ticket."

"I don't believe that. This is somethin' your daddy cooked up, isn't it?"

"No, Mama. Like I said, this person bought me a ticket after I told her Daddy needed me and I was goin' to him any way I could."

"Is he drunk?"

"No. We're fixin' supper. We just been to the grocery."

"Marble, I'm glad you're safe, but why didn't you leave me a note? Or call? Somethin'!"

"You woulda come after me, is why. I was gonna write you a letter tomorrow."

"Let me talk to your daddy again."

"Yes, Bird," said Wes.

"You have that girl on a bus or a plane by tomorrow afternoon or I swear, Wesson Lesson, Fernando will have your red ass in jail by evenin'."

"Bird?"

"What?"

"Let her stay here a spell. I'll see she goes back soon, I promise."

"Wesson, she's got to go to school here. And your promises ain't worth a shit."

"One week, Bird. I swear, Marble'll be there in a week. A few days won't make no difference to the school. Marble wouldn'ta come if it weren't important to her."

"If you put a mark on her, I'll kill you myself. You hear?"

"I'm not drinkin' now, not with Marble by me.

Thanks, Bird. This means a lot to me and her both."

"Put her back on."

"Mama, I'm stayin'."

"Just for the week, Marble."

Marble did not respond.

"Marble! You there?"

"Yes, Mama."

"Did you hear what I said? One week."

"I heard you, Mama. Look, I've got to get things goin' here. Sorry I caused you to worry."

"Sorry ain't the half of it."

"Bye, Mama," Marble said, and hung up.

She turned toward her father, who was standing next to the sink, looking out the kitchen window into the backyard.

"Daddy?"

"Yes, Marble?"

"Why did you beat on Mama all those times?"

"Because I was sick. Sick and ignorant, too. There's nothin' I ever can say or do will make it right. Your mama's gone from me, honey, as she should be. I'm lucky she didn't shoot me dead. Or at least allow me to choke to death on my own vomit, like she mighta did lots of times."

Wes went over to Marble and hugged her to him.

"Marble, your mama's right about my promises ain't bein' worth a shit, but I'm determined to straighten up my life. I'm just pleased to have you bear witness to my determination."

The doorbell rang.

"I'll get it, Daddy."

Marble went to the front door, opened it, and saw a gigantic, moon-faced man wearing a pink Hawaiian shirt decorated with yellow parrots.

"Evenin', miss. My name is Defillo Humble and I'm lookin' for the gentleman of the house. He in?"

"Daddy!" Marble yelled.

Wes Lesson came to the door.

"You lookin' a whole day's pay better'n you did the other night," said Defillo Humble.

"You the fella brought me home?"

Humble nodded. "Just checkin' back, like I said I would. See how you doin'."

"Come in, Mr. — ?"

"Humble. Defillo Humble. Call me Humble, even if I ain't."

He laughed and entered. The two men shook hands.

"I'm Wes Lesson, Humble. Thanks for the act of mercy. Hope I'll never need another for the same reason. This is my daughter, Marble."

Defillo Humble smiled. He had huge yellow teeth.

"You're very large, Mr. Humble," said Marble.

"In most ways," he said. "In others, not nearly large enough for some."

"Would you like to join us for supper?" asked Wes. "We were just about to prepare somethin'."

"Obliged, but I can't. Take a rain check, though. Say, Wes, are you by any chance lookin' for work?"

"As a matter of fact, I am."

"Got a call from an old buddy of mine needs help. Here's his card."

Humble took a card out of his breast pocket and

handed it to Wes, who read it aloud.

" 'Bunk Colby's Balloon and Airship Academy. Cuba, Alabama. Telephone 205-FLY HIGH.' "

"Like I say, he's an old pal. Place is across the state line from Meridian, Mississippi. Needs a man has some mechanical skills."

"I worked in the oil fields, and I can change a tire," said Wes, "but I don't have any aeronautical knowledge."

"Don't need any. That's Bunk's concern. Listen, I'm drivin' up to see Bunk tomorrow. Why don't you come with me, check it out? Bring Marble along."

"Why not, Daddy? You got to make a change."

Defillo Humble bestowed upon her another xanthic caterpillar of a grin.

"I'll be by at ten in the mornin'," Humble said, and let himself out.

"This might could be a good thing, Daddy. The Lord works in mysterious ways."

Wes inspected the card again, then looked at his daughter.

"You're right, Marble," he said. "Let's hope real hard, though, that it's the Lord who's doin' this job of work."

GOOD PEOPLE

"What about Bunk?" asked Wes, as Defillo Humble headed his Roadmaster northeast on 59. They had just crossed the Pearl River into the Magnolia State. Wes was up in front with Humble, and Marble had fallen asleep in the back seat.

"What about him?" said Humble. "You mean, what type fella is he?"

"Yeah. How long has he been operatin' this school? Who goes there? Cuba, Alabama, ain't exactly conveniently located."

"Well, I tell you, Wes, Bunk has did a bunch in his lifetime, which is now closin' on seventy-five years. Thing is, before this deal, he ain't really made any what I call decent money."

"There that many people want to learn how to fly balloons and blimps?"

Humble laughed. "Your girl sleepin'?"

Wes looked at Marble. "Yes."

"What Bunk's got is an airfield, a landin' strip. The balloon academy is just a cover for the real business, which is flyin' in drugs from Central America, mostly grass and cocaine from the Guajira Peninsula in Colombia. Eighty percent of the marijuana smuggled into the United States is grown and shipped from there. The *marimberos* bring it up, pay off Bunk for the use of his strip, where the shit's unloaded and picked up, then they take off again. Bunk don't have nothin' to do with the distribution itself. He needs a man to help keep things runnin' smooth. Bunk knows everything there is to know about airplanes. He was a pilot in WW Two, again in Korea, flew for TWA for fifteen years, then piloted private jets for Sheik Majeed out of Abu Dhabi for a couple."

"You don't mind my askin', don't the fact you don't know hardly a thing about me bother you? I mean, tellin' me about this operation and takin' me to the location? What makes you think I might not go to the authorities with this information?"

Humble showed his yellow teeth to the incisors. "You even considered doin' that, Wes, Marble back there would be a memory. I like to believe I got pretty fair intuition about people, though. You're not the talkin' type, I don't reckon."

Wes stared out the passenger-side window at the gray sky. The temperature outside was in the low forties and heavy rains were expected by nightfall.

"How do you figure into the deal, Humble?"

"I'm kind of an investor, you might say. A stockholder

in the Academy. Helped old Bunk get the thing orga-
nized usin' some of the proceeds from my first book,
Negroes with Cars. You might not completely recall my
tellin' you about it bein' a best-seller, since you was
pretty well inebriated at the time. Writin's my main
occupation, but a wise man doesn't ignore his invest-
ments. Diversification's the name of the game, Wes. I'm
there for Bunk when he needs me."

The drive to Cuba took about four hours. Marble slept
practically the entire way, and Wes, after learning the
true nature of Bunk Colby's business, kept the conversation with Defillo Humble to a minimum, half-pretending
to doze off. A mile or two past Cuba, which was something less than a whistle-stop of a town, Humble turned
south on a dirt road through farmland.

"This is where they grow Silver Queen corn," he said,
"the best there is. Nothin' like Silver Queen corn from
'Bama, boy. Mm-mm! Look on ahead there, Wes. See it?"

Arced over the dirt road was a white entrance
sign: **BUNK COLBY'S BALLOON & AIRSHIP ACADEMY,**
painted in large black block letters. Below that was
written, *"May the curse of God fall on those evil dwarfs."*

As the big blue Buick passed under the arch and clat-
tered toward the Butler building that stood adjacent to
an airplane runway, Wes asked, "Who's the quotation
from?"

Humble chuckled. "Bunk stuck that on durin' the Per-
sian Gulf War. It's what Saddam Hussein said just after
commencin' 'the mother of all battles.' There're folks
think Bunk's sense of humor's more'n some strange, but
he's always been good people to me."

BUNK

"T"he first thing Wes Lesson noticed about Bunk Colby was that he resembled a cat. This is not the face of a seventy-five-year-old man, Wes thought, as he and Marble followed Defillo Humble to where Bunk was standing. The former fighter, airline and Arabian potentate's pilot-turned-drug smuggler was tying a knot in the rigging of a hot-air balloon that was anchored between the Butler building and the airstrip. It was the only balloon on the property, and Wes did not see any blimps, only a Piper Cub painted entirely black parked on the opposite side of the strip. Bunk completed the knot and stepped forward to greet the trio.

"Humble, you're a man of your word," he said, shaking hands with the big guy.

"Try to be," said Defillo Humble. "This here's Wes Lesson and his daughter, Marble. Folks, meet the legend

himself, Bunk Colby, the terror of three or more conti-
nents."

"Only four," Bunk said. "Glad to meet you both." He
shook hands with Wes and Marble.

"Bunk, I swear, you look younger every time I see
you," said Humble.

Bunk smiled, showing a row of sparkling white caps.

"Yeah, this new face surgeon I got down in Bogotá
knows how to handle a parin' knife. Think maybe he
stretched the skin too tight this time, tucked too much
behind my ears. Makes me look like a cat. What do you
think? I look like a cat?"

"It'll loosen up, Bunk," Humble said. "Shake down
some, like always. Besides, the Egyptians worshipped
cats."

"You can stick the Egyptians where the sun don't
shine, far as I'm concerned," said Bunk. "Pardon me,
little lady, don't mean to offend. But they're mighty
unpleasant people to do business with. Filthy, too. Lost
my first set of false teeth in a hotel room in Cairo. Build-
in' caught fire middle of the night and I had to leave 'em
behind. You remember, Humble. My third wife, Nazli,
burned to death in that fire. Only been married thirteen
days. I got all the way downstairs before I remembered
her hands were still tied to the bedposts, and then there
was too much smoke for me to go back after her. Terrible
way to die, don't you think? She wasn't much older'n
this girl here. How old are you, darlin'?"

"Fourteen," said Marble. "How old are you?"

"Fifty-six," said Bunk, winking. "Had my age lowered
in Bogotá, too."

Humble laughed. "Bunk, pretty quick you'll be younger than me."

Bunk's face turned serious, his eyes disappearing. "You tell this fella the score?"

Humble nodded and both he and Bunk looked at Wes.

"Need a man here maybe twelve, fifteen days a month," Bunk said. "You're from New Orleans, huh?"

"Livin' there now," said Wes.

"I pay good and I'll give you a vehicle to use you can drive back and forth from New Orleans between delivery periods. All you have to do is be ready with a wrench and give the appearance of knowin' which end of the AK-47 you're holdin' deals the cards. Well, you people must be hungry. Come on inside. I got some *menudo* mumblin' on the stove."

After they all had eaten, Humble and Bunk had some business to discuss, so Wes and Marble took a walk around the grounds of the Academy.

"Daddy, are you gonna go to work for that man?"

"I'm not sure what I'll do, Marble. There's not much shakin' job-wise in N.O., that's certain. Bunk's kind of money's nothin' to sneeze at."

"I don't think I like him, Daddy. Defillo Humble, neither. They're weird men."

Wes half-laughed. "They sure are."

Later that afternoon, the four of them drove into Meridian in Humble's Buick Roadmaster to see a movie and have dinner. The choice of films was not extensive. It was either a re-release of Disney's *101 Dalmatians* or a new karate-cop picture, *Showdown in Little Tokyo*. The men left the decision to Marble, who said she had seen

101 Dalmatians three times, so they went to the other one, which turned out to be pretty bad.

Over ribs in the T for Texas Barbecue, Bunk agreed with Humble that the movie wasn't very deep.

"Bullets, breasts and decapitation ain't enough to carry a picture," said Bunk. "My favorite's still *Hail the Conquering Hero,* where Eddie Bracken gets mistaken for a war hero by his hometown and all hell breaks loose. It's crazy but human crazy, you know what I mean? Movie like the one we seen just now is devoid of humanity."

"Way the world is, Bunk," said Humble. "Humanity's had its day. Appears our best times been and gone."

"But Marble here has her best times in front of her," Bunk said, smiling at the girl. "In fact, they're comin' right up. Ain't that so, Marble's daddy?"

Wes said, "I hope to hell, Bunk. I really do."

Marble said nothing.

THE BLINK OF AN EYE

Humble, Wes and Marble accepted Bunk's invitation to stay overnight at the Academy and return the next morning to New Orleans. On the ride back to Cuba from Meridian, Wes told Bunk that he would take the job but that he could not begin for a week, until Marble left for Jacksonville, and Bunk said that was all right by him. There was a small dormitory-type setup at the rear of the fifteen-thousand-square-foot Butler building, the remainder of which was divided into office and warehouse space, so guest accommodations were not a problem.

Once they were inside, Bunk noticed that the red light was flashing on his answering machine. He hit the message button.

"Black zero, black zero. Straight up, straight up. Hammerhead, hammerhead. Respond, Cuba, respond."

Bunk immediately punched up a number on the telephone and as soon as his connection was made, he said, "Cuba big, Cuba big. Lay down, black zero. Lay down, black zero. Zero in."

He hung up and told Defillo Humble, "Got a unexpected visitor comin' in at midnight. Better tell Lesson to put his kid to bed. I've got to set the lights."

At one minute past midnight, Humble, Wes and Bunk stood next to the landing strip watching a Learjet taxi toward them. The airplane stopped and idled while the passenger door opened and an aluminum stepladder was lowered to the ground. A man wearing light but sturdy casual clothing, dressed as if he were going sailing, and carrying a green duffel bag, climbed down the ladder, put the duffel on the ground, then lifted the ladder back into the plane. The man picked up the duffel bag and walked toward the reception committee as the jet taxied toward the far end of the runway. Bunk stepped forward to greet the visitor.

"Bienvenida, Señor de Estoques," said Bunk. "It's been a pretty little while."

They did not shake hands but the man, a handsome, clean-shaven Latino in his mid-twenties, smiled at Bunk, then turned and watched the Learjet rumble away, ascend in the north and describe a perfect 180° arc before disappearing into the sub-tropical moonlit sky.

"Mozo, this is Defillo Humble, a longtime associate," Bunk said, "and Wes Lesson, my new assistant. Gentlemen, meet Mozo de Estoques, from Medellín, a most highly valued member of the Colombian Boys Club."

Mozo de Estoques smiled again and spoke in close-to-perfect English.

"Señor Bunk, how can it be that you look younger

now than you did when I first met you? That was what,
eleven years ago? I was fourteen then."

"I remember. It was in Cali, and you'd just completed
your first assignment for the Club."

"Broke my cherry, as you *norteamericanos* say."

Bunk nodded. "That's right. Mozo was no bigger'n
your little girl sleepin' inside, Wes, when he embarked
on his illustrious career. Just a kid."

"What little girl?" asked Mozo de Estoques.

"Wes's daughter," said Bunk. "She's asleep back in
the dormitory."

"How old is she?"

"I don't know," Bunk said. "Twelve or thirteen."

"She's fourteen," said Wes. "What difference does it
make?"

Mozo looked at Wes Lesson, reflections from the runway lights flickering like tiny flames in the Colombian's
unblinking black eyes. He smiled with the corners of his
mouth.

"Much," said de Estoques. "It makes much difference."

"Come on, men, let's go inside," said Bunk. "Take 'em
back, Humble, while I kill these lights. Be right there."

Humble and Wes walked behind Mozo, who obviously
had been there before. He tossed down his duffel bag and
went into the restroom.

"Who is he?" Wes asked Humble.

"Jorge Muleta's top assassin. He's here to hit somebody big, you can bet. Mozo de Estoques don't travel for
no good reason. He supposedly whacked the last two
opposition presidential candidates down there. Runs a

school for assassins financed by the Muleta cartel."

Bunk came in at the same time as Mozo emerged from the can.

"How much time you got, son?" Bunk asked him.

"A car will come in three hours or less. I'm tired, Señor Bunk." Mozo yawned and stretched his arms and back. He studied his oversized Rolex. "If I am still asleep at two forty-five, wake me up."

"You got it."

The assassin picked up his bag and headed for the dormitory.

"How about a drink, Bunk?" said Humble. "Got any of that Glenmorangie left?"

The three men were perched on stools around a stainless steel table in the kitchen area. Bunk and Humble were sipping single-malt Scotch and Wes held a can of Dr Pepper.

"Only time I was in Colombia," Bunk said, "Estrago Muleta—that's Jorge's younger brother who was executed by a firin' squad year before last in Venezuela, Maracaibo, I believe—he and I were out in the jungle when we come upon the biggest goddamn snake I've ever saw, sleepin' smack in the middle of the trail. Estrago said it was a bushmaster, a *serpiente muy peligroso*. Estrago handed me his Uzi machine pistol and snuck up on the viper, lopped off its head with a machete. Reptile didn't budge. Estrago hoisted the head on the tip of his long knife and carried it that way, like a Sioux with Custer's scalp, back to the camp. Boy was one fearless son of a bitch. Well, he's a government footnote now."

The gunshot came before the scream. There was a very loud pop that sounded like a deeply imbedded cork being removed from a goosenecked bottle, followed by Marble's long, wobbly howl. Wes was the first of the three men to reach her. Marble sat on the floor next to the cot on which she had been sleeping, clasping in her two hands a Colt Python pointed at the inert body of Mozo de Estoques, who lay draped across the cot, naked from the waist down, except for his white cotton socks.

Wes took the pistol from his daughter, who sat perfectly still, rigid, her eyes frozen open. He knelt next to Marble and hugged her to him. Humble pushed aside Mozo's black forelock, revealing reddish ooze where his right eye had been. Bunk came in last, took a look at the scene, started to say something, then stopped. Wes gently caressed his daughter's head as he held her, and after a minute or two, she blinked.

STICKING WITH JESUS

Dear Jesus,

It has been a while since I wrote I know but lots has happened during this time. I will begin with the big event and go back. I killed a man who tried to rape me in Alabama. You know I am fourteen and still a virgin child and intend to remain one until I decide to do it though I have to tell you not necessarily in the marriage bed. Anyway that is the big news now I will tell you how it happened.

Daddy and I went with a stranger named Defillo Humble to see about a job for Daddy at an airfield in Alabama by the border of Mississippi. This stranger had helped out Daddy I guess when he was drunk in trouble one night and when he showed back up at the house and said he might know about a job Daddy figured why not check it out due to his not having one and the work *situation in his home state of Louisiana not being good at the moment. I did not have a very good feeling about this man Humble who is an extremely large person but who says he is a writer which did interest me. As you know I have ambitious desires in that direction.*

So we went with Defillo Humble in his Buick up around Meridian to this airfield which is a school called Bunk Colby's Balloon and Airship Academy. It is run by an extremely strange man Bunk Colby who says he is 75 years old but looks almost as young as Daddy. There was one balloon there but nothing else of an air nature that I could see. This school was way out in nowhere and I did not think Daddy would accept work there but he did being so desperate and not drinking though he is not going to work there now of course.

That night we were there was when everything happened. Mr. Humble, Mr. Colby and Daddy and I went to Meridian to eat dinner and see a movie called Showdown in Little Tokyo. The dinner was OK at a barbecue restaurant but the movie was dumb and awful with really fake looking foot fighting, automatic weapons galore going off, and lots of naked women with mostly Japanese criminals. The worst part was where the leader of the Japanese criminals cuts off the head of a blond woman with a sword in one hand while he rubs her bare breasts with his other. He does this from behind her with no shirt on so we can see he is tattooed all over his chest and shoulders and arms and stomach. Later he is killed but you would not believe how horrible this movie is Jesus don't go see it.

After we got back to Mr. Colby's place I went to sleep

in a room with lots of small beds in it because it was too late to drive all the way back to New Orleans. I woke up with a man on top of me I did not know who he was. He put a hand over my mouth and pulled down my blanket with his other to get at me. I turned my head and saw a gun on the floor next to the bed and while he was doing things to himself I reached down and grabbed the gun and put the nose by the side of his face and pulled the trigger.

The man collapsed on me and there was junk everywhere not just blood but stuff from inside his head. I guess I screamed then and crawled out from under his body and would have shot him again if he moved but he was completely dead and did not. Daddy came and held me. I knew it was him but honest Jesus I could not talk or even move for a long time. Mr. Humble and Mr. Colby came in and saw the mess but they did not say a word.

Daddy held me in the back seat of Mr. Humble's car all the way back to New Orleans in the middle of the night. I guess Mr. Colby buried the body of the rapist who Daddy told me later was a murderer from South America who the U.S. government was after and would be glad to know he was dead but we were not going to tell them or anybody else. I promised Daddy I would not tell Mama about any of this because she would never allow me to visit Daddy again not that she wanted me to anyway as you know. But I had to tell you Jesus you are the only one.

I am writing this on the bus back to Florida. Remember the last time I was on it a bolt of lightning hit us and every passenger except me was killed or hurt bad. I know for certain now that I was spared for a special purpose and probably for more than one. The first was to destroy the South American killer and rapist who beyond any doubt in my mind was an agent of the devil. More are out there Jesus and I am ready for them. There is a TV show that says 25 million people claim to have spoken with the devil and I believe it. I also believe there are others on the planet such as myself who can save the world from the devil and his agents. Stick close with me Jesus I am on your side forever.

Your friend,

Marble Lesson

ABOUT THE AUTHOR

Barry Gifford was born on October 18, 1946, in Chicago, Illinois, and raised there and in Key West and Tampa, Florida. He has received awards from PEN, the National Endowment for the Arts, the Art Directors Club of New York and the American Library Association. His writing has appeared in *Punch, Esquire, Cosmopolitan, Rolling Stone, Sport,* the *New York Times,* the *New York Times Book Review* and many other publications. Mr. Gifford's books have been translated into fifteen languages, and his novel *Wild at Heart* was made into an award-winning film by David Lynch. He lives in the San Francisco Bay Area.